WHAT OTHERS ARE SAYING
ABOUT SKY ALEXANDER

The Fires of Love & Hate" is a sweeping historical saga!
—**Pam Brewer,** *The Idaho Statesman*

Great historical family drama

5 Stars!

I loved reading. So, One day I found this book by chance. I read this very carefully. WOW.....Nice one. As well as, this book is easy reading to anyone. The author has used simple sentences. Therefore, you can understand the story. But, his writing is deep and emotional putting me right in the middle of the Western Romance that he has written. So, I like to his writing style. Highly recommend.....!!!
-Thashmira H., Amazon review

A really great book!

This historical romance book looked like a really great story so I decided to buy it. When I began to read it I instantly fell in love with the book, it's written so beautifully and I got gripped on the story. It really reminded me of classics such as 'gone with the wind' and other great ones. The western romance between a girl and a boy was unstoppable to read, I really enjoyed reading their journey. I highly recommend this book if you love classics, a good love story or just looking for a great read. The story truly captured me.
-Russell B., Amazon review

Intriguing, Gut-Wrenching, Volatile, Captivating!

I just finished reading this book and...WOW! Awesomely gut
wrenching & beautiful all at the same time!

I am very excited to be a part of this series with Urban Talent in
the ways that I am & I can't wait to get the rest of these books done
& in your hands!!

—Bailey Heesch

Great historical family drama

The Fires of Love and Hate is historical and family drama novel
and it is the first in the series of novels about Hattie, an author's
great-grandmother. The story of Hattie begins to take place in nineteenth century with her forced marriage and continues with how she
deals with this tough situation.

The story is based on some real characters and actual events and
that is what makes it even more interesting to read. Also, the book
is well written, it is inspiring, easy to read and it really draws you into
it.

I highly recommend it to any fan of family, romance or historical
genre.

—Yania, Amazon review

An inspiring read with strong female characters

Sky Alexander's "The Fires of Love and Hate" tells the story of
how a strong woman deals with an unwanted arranged marriage in
nineteenth century America.

The novel, inspired by the author's family stories, is set in small-town Missouri, when the state's biggest wedding is about to take place.

I really enjoyed the characterization of the protagonist, strong-willed bride-to-be, Hattie Morran, whose poor father has offered her to be married to the cruel Abner Garland as payment for gambling debts.

Although Hattie is livid she is forced to marry someone she hates, she plans a way to gain the upper hand in the situation, which eventually results in her becoming extraordinarily wealthy.

"The Fires of Love and Hate" has a few underlying themes, the main ones being optimism, perseverance, and faith.

One of the strengths of the novel is the interesting dialogue, which is both engaging and realistic.

I feel the hands-down strongest feature of the novel is its cast of strong female characters. Regardless of the trials set in front of them, they remain determined and optimistic.

Overall, I found the book to be an inspiring, interesting read that is perfect for anyone interested in the historical-romance genre. I can't wait for the next book in the series!

—Rich Blaisdell

Great read!!

This book was great! Captivates you at the beginning and you find you can't put it down! You feel like you are right there with the characters. Loved it!

—Jo

The Fires of Love and Hate

This book is easy reading and becomes hard to put down as you get pulled into the lives of each character. You will find yourself rooting for Hattie and her family as they overcome the many trials life has in store for them. I loved the body guards! Especially Matthew! I can't wait to read the sequel!

—**Theatre Girl**

DEATH OF LOVE

Book 4 in The Fires of Love & Hate Series

SKY ALEXANDER

First eBook Edition: 2015
ISBN: 978-0-9915836-6-9
First Paperback Edition 2015
ISBN: 978-0-9915836-7-6

The characters and events portrayed in this book are fictitious. Any similarity to a real person, living or dead, is coincidental and not intended by the author.

Falling into Love: a novel/by Sky Alexander

Cover design by © StoneHouse Ink

Published in the United States of America

"Sometimes the worst thing that happens - is also the best."
~ Naomi Judd

Acknowledgments

I, Sky Alexander, would like to acknowledge first, Heavenly Father from whom all of my inspiration comes from. Secondly, my Father Shayne Bryan Alexander, who originally had the dream to write a series that, could help to encourage people through his writing and give some light to them in the darkest times of their lives. Thirdly, my great grandmother Hattie who truly lived such a colorful life, which I would have a basis to draw from and without her there, would never have been a story to write. She was truly a woman born years ahead of her time with selfless acts of kindness and grace inspired not only those around her but her children and her children's children to this very day.

Finally I would like to acknowledge my family and friends who have supported me in the endeavor to finish my father's work and to see things through in my life's dream to be a well renowned author and like my father share from my own ideas and experience with others to help them focus and pursue their dreams. Without their help, I think I never would have seen days like these.

Preface

Throughout history, few women have had the money and power to make a substantial difference for good in the lives of others. When great wealth and power have been within their grasp, unbridled greed, passion, and ambition have usually walked hand in hand with them. Yet, scattered throughout the ages, truly great women have been born who, because of their very nature, rise above their circumstances and spend their lives trying to lift people to a higher level of understanding by their essence of pure unselfish love. The young Hattie Morran was one such woman, and this is her story.

Chapter 1
COLLISION COURSE WITH LOVE

DURING THE WEEKS FOLLOWING Newton's funeral, Hattie looked for anything to take her mind off of Ira. To fill the long days, Hattie divided her time between her endless business ventures, getting to know Lorna and her children, and spending time with little Katherine. It seemed like a perfect routine, but once the days ended, Hattie was once again left alone with her thoughts in the still of night. The same noises of the night that she had grown up loving so much now seemed eerily deafening. Sleep, which used to be so peaceful and rejuvenating, was now nearly impossible, and to make matters worse, when she did manage to sleep, she seemed to awaken constantly.

Through it all, though, Minerva was amazed at Hattie's perseverance, as she continued to visit Ira regularly at the jail to try and brighten his days. With little hope of being cleared of Nick's murder, Ira turned deep within himself to hide the pain and guilt he was feeling. The many evils of his life had caught up with him, and for Ira, it was almost too much to bear.

Seeing his increasingly despondent behavior, Hattie encouraged him to write the story of his life. "Besides giving you something to do," she said compassionately, "it will give you an opportunity to tell your side of the story." Handing him some writing materials, she continued. "This is your chance to get out all the pain, hurt, and frustration you've been holding inside. Sometimes," she added with a smile, "all it takes to feel better is to vent a little. Whether you yell, cry, pray, talk to someone, or write is immaterial. What is important is that you don't continue to become bitter by holding things inside."

Nodding his head, Ira knew Hattie was right, and even though he didn't want to, he took the writing materials and began to write.

When she wasn't busy with James, Lorna, or Ira, Hattie could undoubtedly be found sketching. Her grandfather, Elijah, had taught her the skill when she was very young, and through the years, she had become quite proficient at it. More than that, though, it was her favorite stress-relieving activity, and with more uncertainty in her life now than ever before, Hattie spent countless hours at her easel.

One unusually warm day near the end of October, Hattie decided to get out of the house and go down to the creek to sketch. Matthew walked with her carrying Katherine, while the rest of the men followed closely behind. Once they arrived near the water's edge, Matthew laid out a big blanket and played with Katherine, while Hattie stood at her easel and poured herself into a new drawing. After about an hour, the peace and quiet that they had been enjoying was broken when Cameron's voice called out to Hattie from the clearing heading back to the mansion. Looking up from her work, she saw him approaching with someone.

"Hattie," Cameron called out again as he got closer, "you have a visitor."

Seeing Chandra Spalding emerge from the clearing, Hattie immediately stopped what she was doing and went to meet her. "Chandra? Is that really you?" She asked, amazed.

"Surprise!" Chandra replied excitedly.

"What are you doing here?"

"It's a long story actually, but since I was passing through Gallatin, I knew that I couldn't leave without stopping to say hello."

Turning to Matthew and Cameron, Hattie knew that introductions were necessary. "Matthew, Cameron, this is Chandra Spalding, now a teacher for the Vassar College in New York, and Chandra, these men are two of my bodyguards, Matthew and Cameron Forsythe."

Blushing slightly while both Matthew and Cameron took a turn kissing her hand, Chandra couldn't help but smile. In all her twenty-four years, she had never seen men as handsome as these two tall, dark-haired wonders. Fanning herself with her hand, Chandra said, "It is very nice to meet you Matthew. I was fortunate enough to make Cameron's acquaintance already, but a formal introduction is nice none the less."

"Chandra was one of the girls who Rebecca hired to teach me and the family how to speak and act correctly," Hattie told Matthew and Cameron as the four of them sat on boulders by the creek. "She and some other girls from the college stayed with us for a spell a couple of years ago, and it is because of their intense courses on etiquette that I am the lady I am today."

"Hattie, please," Chandra replied modestly, "it had little to do with us. You are a natural. All you needed was a push in the right direction."

"So, honestly Chandra, what brings you to town? I mean, it's not everyday someone from back east comes to Gallatin, Missouri."

"Well, as I said in my last telegram several months ago, I am now a teacher for Vassar. It is a great honor, to be sure, but along with that honor, there are a great many responsibilities. One of them happens to be that I am required to attend meetings in places all over the country on women's rights. This semester's meetings were in Chicago, but before heading back to the college, I also have business in Kansas City, which, as luck would have it, just happened to bring me through Gallatin. So, like I said before, there was no way I was going to miss visiting you when I was so close."

"Oh, and I'm so glad you did," Hattie replied enthusiastically.

"So am I, but as wonderful as it is to see you, I'm afraid I can't stay long. Because of the business I have yet to tend to, I need to be back on the train early tomorrow morning."

"Well, short visit or not," Hattie responded cheerfully, "seeing you is exactly what I needed to take my mind off of things."

"Yes, about that, Hattie. Back at the house, Minerva was kind enough to fill me in on everything that has happened since your last telegram. I want you to know that if you ever need any help with anything from me or the college, I promise you that I will do all that I can."

Touched by Chandra's kind words, Hattie didn't know what to say. She knew all too well that true friends were hard to come by, but just hearing the sincerity in her voice, Hattie could sense that Chandra was of those rare people that would stand by a friend no matter what. Sitting in silence for several seconds, Hattie finally turned to Cameron and said, "Cameron, please send someone to the house to tell Mary that we will be having company for dinner."

"Yes, Ma'am."

"And tell her to fix something extra special," Hattie added firmly, "Chandra will only be here for a short time, so I want that time to be the best it can possibly be."

"Absolutely," Cameron said, as he hurried away.

During the next hour, Chandra and Hattie talked extensively about everything under the sun. They found that even though they were several years apart in age, they still had many things in common. Chandra even looked like Hattie in many regards. They were about the same height, they both carried themselves with the utmost of class and dignity, and they both dressed exquisitely. Chandra's brown hair was a bit longer than Hattie's auburn red hair and their eyes were different color, but other than that, the two women had very similar looks.

Standing by the creek, their conversation fell on the subject of women. Admiring the sparkling blue water as it ran lazily ran down stream, they spoke of their own futures as leaders and contributors to society. Finally, picking up a dead leaf, Chandra said, "You know what, Hattie?"

"No, what?"

"Your problems are like many of those of the Dean at Vassar, having both been born years before your time. You really must come there and visit with her and the professors, as they find you fascinating, and your generous donations have been greatly appreciated. Most of all, though, I think that you would find comfort being with women of your own strength and character."

Playing with the idea in her head, Hattie sighed heavily. "One day, when Ira is no longer my priority, I just might do that."

Chandra understood Hattie's reluctance perfectly, and deciding not to push the issue, she walked over to Hattie's easel and looked at her work. On the pad was a sketch of Hattie beside a beautiful stream and a grove of trees. In the background was a large mansion, surrounded by high canyon walls. "Is that somewhere you've been?" Chandra asked, curious.

Smiling, Hattie replied, "No, but strangely enough, it's a place I've often seen in my dreams. In the beginning, it was just a fleeting glimpse here and there, but I've dreamed of it so often lately that I was finally able to put it all together, creating what you see in front of you. It's becoming so vivid in my mind, I'm afraid it's becoming an obsession."

Leaning forward, Chandra looked closer at the drawing. "I can see why. This mansion is hauntingly beautiful and unlike anything I've ever seen."

"If I ever find that place, I'll build that mansion exactly as I have envisioned it in my mind. And Chandra," Hattie added emphatically, "it will be magnificent!" Reaching out for Chandra's hand, Hattie encouraged her to follow her. "Come, let's walk for a spell. I want to enjoy what's left of the fall colors on the trees." Calling to Matthew, who was about twenty feet away tending to Katherine, Hattie said, "Matthew, would you have one of the men take Katherine and my things back to the house?"

"Sure."

"And after you're done, please come and walk with us."

Matthew stood, brushed off his pants, and called to several men who were out of sight. After passing on to them Hattie's instructions, he hurriedly caught up with the women. Reaching them, Hattie held out her hand, and he took it. Together, the three of them walked along the creek in the warm sunshine, as a light breeze scattered the dead leaves in front of their feet. Turning around to make sure that several men were following them, he said, "It's awfully nice to be with you ladies this afternoon, Miss Hattie."

"So, do you like your job, Matthew?" Chandra asked politely.

"Is Salt Lake in the mountains?" he replied playfully. "Of course I love my job. Who wouldn't?" Then, with sudden seriousness in his voice, he turned to Hattie and asked, "Hattie, do you mind if I ask you for a favor?"

"Sure, but whatever it is, you've got it."

"But you don't even know what it is yet."

"It doesn't matter, Matthew. If you want it, you got it."

Shaking his head, Matthew turned to Chandra with a smile. "You see what I mean. She is amazing. I could not find a better job if I looked for an eternity." Pausing, Matthew walked along in silence for several seconds. "Could I at least tell you what it is I want, Hattie?"

"Oh all right," Hattie replied, laughing.

"I'd like for you to interview my younger brother, Archer. George Hightower is wanting to return home to Salt Lake City soon, and we'll need a replacement for him."

"Oh, I hate to lose George, but if you'd like to have your brother take his place, he doesn't need an interview with me. Send for him immediately. Your recommendation is more than enough."

"Great!" Matthew replied. "He'll be here tomorrow. Are you interested in knowing anything about him?"

"How good is he with a gun?"

"Top notch. He's been practicing ever since the rest of us came to work for you. He may be even quicker and better than I am."

Hattie smiled. Matthew certainly wasn't conceited, so if he said that Archer was good, he meant it. "Then the matter is settled, Matthew. Hire him when he arrives."

"That's it. Don't you want to know anything else about him?"

"Okay, how old is he?"

"Eighteen; and he's already aware of how dangerous this job can be."

"Well, if he's aware of the danger involved, capable of doing the job, and is agreeable, he's hired." Looking into his eyes, Hattie could see how important this was to him. "Everyone should be as lucky to have an older brother like Matthew," she thought.

Turning her attention to Chandra, Hattie said, "The reason I wanted to walk was so that I could ask you something."

"What is it?"

"First of all, I want you to know what a wonderful time I've had this afternoon. This time that we've had together to talk is exactly what I needed."

"I've had a wonderful time too, Hattie. What are you trying to get at?"

"Well, I would like for us to be able to spend more time together. I know that during the school year you're very busy, but if you would like, I would love to have you come and stay with me during the summers. What do you think?"

"I would love too," Chandra replied, flattered. "I don't have anything to hold me in New York during the summers, and it would be fun spending that time with you."

"The only thing is I'm considering leaving Gallatin when this ordeal with Ira is over. Would you be willing to spend the summers with me wherever I might be?"

"Absolutely. Do you have any idea where you plan to go?"

"I'm not sure. Many of the companies Lou and I have are located back east and in the South. James has suggested that we move to New York City, but me, a country girl, living in the big city, I can't imagine it. I think I'd rather die!"

"Did he mean for you to live right in New York City or in the New York countryside? Because New York State has a lot of beautiful countryside."

"I think he means the city. Dakota, Mama, and the boys offered to go with me, but you know that sketch you were admiring? Well, that place exists somewhere. I just know that it does. And before I die, I've got to find it, Chandra."

"Where in the world would you go to look?"

"Because of the hills and canyons, I figure it's got to be farther out west."

Interrupting them with a long low whistle, Matthew said, "That's pretty untamed territory, Miss Hattie."

"I know it, Matthew, but as long as I've got men like you protecting me and my family supporting me, I'm not too worried. I just feel like, as a family, we need to go somewhere else and make a new start. That is, if you and the men would be willing to go, too?"

"You just say the word, and they'll be packed. As for me, I'd follow you to the ends of the earth, Hattie"

Stopping dead in her tracks, Chandra's jaw dropped.

"What in the world is wrong, Chandra?" Hattie asked.

"Matthew, your devotion to Hattie is amazing. Did you really mean what you just said?"

"Every word," he responded without a flinch. "Hattie is no ordinary woman, Chandra. Things are always going to be happening around her, big things, and I, for one, want to be right in the middle of it all."

Hattie squeezed his hand. "What did I ever do to deserve a friend like you, Matthew? You know, sometimes it seems like we've known each other forever."

Squeezing her hand back, Matthew smiled. "I felt the same way about you, Hattie. From the moment I met you, I knew that we were meant to be together."

Watching Matthew and Hattie gaze longingly into each other's eyes, Chandra wondered exactly what kind of love it was that they had for each other. It was obvious to her that their relationship went beyond friendship, but how much further, she didn't know. All she knew was Matthew was the most gorgeous hunk of a man that she had ever seen, and she wasn't going to let the opportunity to get to know him better pass her by.

Yanking on Matthew's arm, she drew his attention away from Hattie. "Hattie, if you don't mind, I'd like to get better acquainted with this good-looking man of yours."

"Oh, really," Hattie replied with a smile.

"Yes, really."

Smiling, Matthew's eyes, those beautiful blue eyes, had a twinkle in them. Laughing slightly, he said, "My goodness, Chandra, are you planning to court me or what?"

"Matthew Forsythe, this is the 20th Century, and we Vassar women believe in taking the bull by the horns." As they walked, Chandra clung to Matthew's arm, and beneath his shirtsleeve, she felt the muscles rippling.

"I'll tell you what, ladies," Matthew said proudly, "it's an honor to have two of the most beautiful women in the state on either arm like this."

"For heaven's sake, don't let Laville hear you say that," Hattie said with a laugh. "She'd have an ever-living fit."

"She is beautiful, I can't refute that," Matthew replied frankly. "But a woman's beauty is only enhanced by her personality, and in that part of Laville's life, she is sadly lacking. I really wish I knew what it would take to bring out the beauty that is locked away somewhere in her soul. I'd do anything in my power to help her become the woman I know she must be deep down inside."

Smiling, Hattie was reminded again why she cared so much about Matthew. He, unlike most people, could look past the exterior of a person and see them for what they could become. As they walked toward the mansion, Hattie wondered what it was about Matthew that enabled him to see in people, what they couldn't see in themselves? Looking up and seeing his glittery smile, she thought to herself, "What are these feelings that I keep having? I know I love Matthew for everything he is and does, but is it possible that I could be falling in love with him?"

Late that night as she lay in bed, Hattie felt, for the first time in months, a peace inside her. She had gained a wonderful new friend in Chandra, and Matthew, her most trusted friend and companion, had promised to follow her to the ends of the earth. Things seemed to finally be falling into place for Hattie, and closing her eyes, she looked forward to the future with renewed hope.

***

THE NEXT MORNING after seeing Chandra off at the train station, Hattie felt a need to visit Ira. So, with time to kill before Matthew's brother, Archer, arrived at noon, Hattie, Matthew, Cameron, and the rest of the men made their way to the jail. The weather was a bit cooler and windier than the day before, but with mostly sunny skies, it was still a far warmer day than what would be expected for the time of year.

Leaving everyone else outside, Hattie made her way to Ira's cell hoping to spend some quality, private time with him, but from the very start of her visit, it was obvious that Ira's heart and mind were preoccupied with far off concerns. He seemed uninterested in anything she had to say, and after nearly an hour of very one-sided conversation, Hattie exited the jail completely frustrated.

"What's wrong?" Matthew asked as he walked to meet her.

"Ira's what's wrong," Hattie replied, agitated. "I know that communication has never been our strong suit, but his silence and disinterest today was eerie." Throwing her hands in the air, she let out a ragged breath. "He just didn't seem to care about anything, least of all me."

Taking Hattie's hand, Matthew tried to console her. "I'm sure he still cares about you, Hattie. I don't think I have to remind you that he is going through an awful lot right now. It is only three weeks until he goes before the Judge again, and with no new evidence, he has no real hope of being cleared. Whether any of us like it, unless a miracle happens, he will hang."

"You're right," Hattie replied in a softened tone. "I don't know how you do it, Matthew, but you always know how to help me make sense of things. The thing is, I was so happy after yesterday, with Chandra having visited and I wanted to extend that happiness to Ira. I know he is going through a lot, but I've always believed that if I could have a positive attitude around people who were feeling bad that somehow my good feelings would rub off on them." Walking away from Matthew, she leaned up against the wall of the jail. "I guess today proves that things don't always work out like we hope."

"Don't get down on yourself, Hattie," Matthew replied as he leaned up against the wall beside her. "At least you try to affect people for good. Most people won't even bother to help someone in need. Personally, I think your genuine love and compassion for people is an inspiration. I know it's made me a better person."

Laughing slightly, Hattie rolled her eyes. "Matthew, Dear, if you were any better a person, you'd be a saint. I highly doubt that you need me for inspiration. Besides, if anybody inspires anybody around here, it's you who inspires me."

Smiling, Matthew gazed at Hattie's auburn hair as it danced lazily in the autumn breeze. Watching her brush the long strands from her beautiful face, he couldn't help but recall the words that his father had told him before he left Salt Lake City to come and work for Hattie.

"Be careful and guard your heart," he told Matthew bluntly. "These photographs of Miss Hattie show her to be very attractive. It may prove to be almost impossible for you to protect and care for a young woman so beautiful and not fall in love with her."

Now, as the memory of his father's wise words came crashing down upon him like a ton of bricks, Matthew realized for the first time that it was too late. He had tried so hard for so long to not let his feelings interfere with his work, but now, looking at the picture of beauty standing in front of him, he was forced to recognize his feelings. He was completely and hopelessly taken with Hattie. She encompassed every wonderful quality that he had ever dreamed in a wife, yet she wasn't a dream; she was very real. "How could I have let my feelings get away from me like this," he thought desperately. Closing his eyes tightly, he didn't know what to do. On one hand, his heart skipped a beat at the thought of her in his arms. Yet, on the other hand, he felt hopelessness.

Even though Hattie's marriage to Ira was for all intents and purposes over, the fact remained that they were still legally married. That coupled with major religious differences, left Matthew questioning his sanity. For the first time in his life, had no idea what he was going to do. He had always prided himself on being strong and in control of himself and his feelings, but every day now, he and Hattie seemed to grow closer and closer. Matthew couldn't help but feel like he was riding a runaway train of emotions where Hattie was concerned, and whether he liked it or not, it was on a 'collision course with love.'

Chapter 2
FATEFUL ENCOUNTERS

"MATTHEW," HATTIE SAID SOFTLY. "Matthew Stuart," Hattie repeated, as she ran her hand back and forth in front of his eyes. "Are you okay? You've been quiet for an awfully long time."

Hearing Hattie's soothing voice, Matthew was catapulted back to reality from his deep thoughts. Staring straight ahead, he didn't know what to say. Hattie's beautiful emerald eyes begged for an answer to his extended silence, but as much as he wanted to tell Hattie exactly how he was feeling, he knew that he couldn't. With Ira's life still hanging in the balance, Matthew concluded that this was the worst possible time for him to be having feelings for Hattie, but as his father said, "Love knows nothing of timing, Matthew. It comes on its own terms, and usually when you least expect it."

"You haven't answered me, Matthew," Hattie said, interrupting his thoughts again. "Is everything okay?"

Resigned to the fact that he could not act upon the emotions inside of him, Matthew took a deep breath and calmly took Hattie's hand in his own. "Yes, everything is fine," he lied. Then, changing the subject and speaking honestly, he said, "I just feel bad about Ira's situation. His life was just beginning when he met Nick, and yet, their one chance meeting was the beginning of the craziness that now sees Ira sitting in a prison cell, awaiting a death that is all but imminent. Whether he really did kill Nick or not, I can't help but feel for him. I hate to see anyone suffer, and the person who you talked to inside that jail this morning, Hattie, is suffering. He, like anyone in that situation, is very frustrated, and I don't blame him."

Touched by Matthew's sincerity, Hattie forgot all about his earlier silence. His kind words were exactly what she needed to hear. Looking up at him graciously, Hattie said, "Thank you, Matthew, for once again correcting my perspective. I hadn't realized it, but I was so frustrated that Ira wouldn't communicate with me that I totally forgot about his feelings in all of this. I agree that he must be going through hell inside of him, and that, more than anything, is why I want him to open up to me. I want to try and help him."

"Sometimes you can't help," Matthew replied solemnly. "He alone has to deal with the consequences of the choices that he has made, and when the time is right, he will open up to someone. You can count on it."

"I really hope you're right, Matthew. I hate to think that Ira will take his secrets to the grave." Letting out a ragged breath, Hattie concluded, "It is really sad to me to know that if Ira had never met Nick, he wouldn't be in the situation he is in today. Their meeting was definitely one of life's 'fateful encounters'."

No sooner had Hattie finished her sentence, when she heard a voice call out to her from the distance. Turning, she was surprised to see Ira's younger cousin, Walker Donovan, walking toward them.

Striding confidently, Walker was the perfect example of tall, dark, and handsome, and his wit and charm were unmatched in all of Gallatin. Standing nearly six foot two, he had coal black hair, dark brown almost black eyes, and a very muscular build, all of which was accented by a devilishly handsome smile. The youngest of the infamous Donovan

Brothers, he and his four siblings were quite the wild bunch, constantly in and out of trouble with the law. Most men disliked their confident style and free spirits, but with the women, they were quite popular to say the least. As Walker drew close to Hattie, her men stealthily fanned out and surrounded him.

"Easy boys," Walker joked as he saw Hattie's men approach. "I come in peace."

Walking towards Walker with Matthew, Hattie called out to her men. "It's okay, fellas. He's no threat, I assure you." It never ceased to amaze Hattie how quickly, and as if out of thin air, her men appeared. They performed their job with such precision and grace that it often left Hattie spellbound. With all the craziness in her life the past couple of years, she appreciated even more the protection that they provided her. Coming to a stop beside Walker, Hattie turned to her men and explained the relationship between them. "Walker and I attended school together most of our lives," she told them matter-of-factly. "His mama, Ira's aunt, was the schoolteacher, and even though we haven't seen much of each other lately, I know that he would never hurt me, would you Walker?"

"Hurt the amazingly beautiful Miss Hattie? I wouldn't think of it." Bowing slightly, he reached out, took Hattie's hand, and kissed it tenderly. "First of all, despite my reputation, I'm really not as bad as people say, but secondly and even more importantly, if I even so much as looked cross at you, Ira would have my head." Pausing, he looked straight into Hattie's emerald green eyes. "I know you two had your troubles, Miss Hattie, but he still talks fondly of you to me. In fact, he told me to tell you last time I visited him that he never meant for any of these crazy things to happen. He just got mixed up with the wrong guy in Nick Starr."

Tearing up slightly, Hattie knew Walker was telling the truth, and though it bothered her that Ira wouldn't tell her things himself, she was glad to hear about his feelings from somebody. Struggling with her emotions, she asked, "Is that why you're here today, to see Ira?"

"Yes, truth be told, it is. He has always been like a big brother to me, and I like to stop in from time to time to see if I can cheer him up. I really hate the way things have turned out. Ira deserved better, and so did you."

"Well, I sure hope that you have better luck with him than I did earlier," Hattie replied solemnly. "He wasn't very responsive, and unless a miracle happens, I fear that it's only going to get worse in the weeks ahead. I really have tried to have faith that somehow everything would work out, but lately I've come to realize that sometimes no matter how much you hope for a certain result to a situation, it isn't always in the cards."

Nodding his head sympathetically, Walker cleared his throat and said, "I really would love to stay and talk some more, but I only have a short time to see Ira today and I don't want to dally." Tipping his hat, he continued, "It sure was nice seeing you again, Miss Hattie. I don't know what the future holds, but I hope that somehow after all this is over, you find happiness in your life. Lord knows, you've gone through hell." Giving her a wink, he walked over to Matthew, pulled him aside, and spoke firmly. "You keep a good eye on that beauty there, Partner. My mother and I think very highly of Miss Hattie, and if anything happens to her, I'll hold you responsible."

"Believe me," Matthew responded unintimidated, "she's in the best of hands."

Tipping his hat a second time, Walker continued on his way past the other bodyguards and into the jailhouse.

Returning to Hattie's side, Matthew put his arm around her. Looking down at her, he couldn't help his curiosity and asked, "What's the real story behind this Walker fella?"

Sighing heavily while they walked to the carriage, Hattie was slow to respond. "To be honest with you, Matthew, I don't rightly know. We used to be pretty close in school and all, but over the last few years, we haven't talked to each other but a handful of times. He's changed a lot. He's not the young, wild boy that I remember. He really has developed into a devilishly handsome man." Pausing, Hattie thought back to the way he had tenderly kissed her hand and the compassion he had used when talking about Ira. It really amazed her how different he had acted. Walker had always been so boisterous, flashy, and rough around the edges. In all the years they had been in school together, Hattie had never seen this new, gentler, caring side of him. Shaking her head, she struggled for answers but couldn't find any.

Calmly waiting for Hattie to continue, Matthew could sense that she was struggling with her feelings. "What's wrong, Hattie?" he asked kindly.

"Do you believe that people can change, Matthew?"

"In theory, I believe that anyone, if they work hard enough, can change, yes, but yet, because we live in a real world and not in a theoretical one, I tend to believe what my mother used to say."

"And what was that?"

"A leopard doesn't change their spots, and a zebra doesn't change their stripes."

"So you're saying no?"

"What I'm saying is that too really and honestly change, a person has to fight the inbred desire to be the way they used to be and replace it with a new stronger desire to be something different. Real change is a constant battle that lasts every minute of every day for the rest of that person's life, and if they let their focus lapse for even one minute, they will invariably revert right back to the way they were. So, given the extreme dedication and determination that it takes to achieve something like this, I believe that very few people can really change. That is why it is so important for parents to teach their children correctly while they are young, because once they grow up it is nearly impossible for them to change."

Taking a deep breath, Matthew searched for an example. "Think of it in terms of moving a tree," he continued. "When the tree is a sapling, you can move it easily from here to there or wherever, and it will adapt and survive. But if you wait too long and the tree grows to maturity, there is nothing you can do to move it. It is so rooted where it is that it can never be moved." Reaching the carriage, he asked, "Does that make sense?"

"Of course it does, Matthew. You always seem to know exactly how to say things so that they make perfect sense. I just wish I could describe Walker's behavior today."

"How does he usually act?"

"Well, you heard him say it himself. His reputation is not the best in the county with him and his brothers always in and out of trouble with the law. Heck, Mama has warned me about the 'infamous' Donavan Brothers many times. But at the same time, his compassion and general kindness today seemed genuine."

"People are strange, Hattie. Ira's being put in jail has probably had a big effect on him, but like I said earlier, it is really hard for people to change, so I would take anything I saw today with a grain of salt until I knew for sure that he was truly different. And always remember, Hattie, people can pretend to be all kinds of things to get what they want."

Nodding, Hattie put her hand in Matthew's and got into the carriage. Matthew followed, and in a matter of minutes they were off to pick up Matthew's brother Archer at the train station.

Upon arriving, Matthew, Cameron, and Hattie waited anxiously outside the station for Archer's train to arrive. Then, at twelve noon, the train pulled in right on schedule, and within no time at all, Archer was stepping off onto the platform.

Seeing him, both Matthew and Cameron waved and yelled vigorously to get his attention. Walking with Hattie to meet him half way, they met their younger brother with loving embraces. "How was your trip, Little Brother," Cameron asked as he patted him on the shoulder.

"It was great," he replied with a relieved smile. "The trip was so long; I'm just thrilled to finally be here." Turning to Hattie, he took off his hat, shook her hand, and bowed slightly. "Miss Hattie, let me say that it is so wonderful to finally meet you. I've been looking forward to joining my brothers as one of your bodyguards for so long that I'm afraid I'm still in shock that I've actually made it."

Taking a step back, Hattie smiled and said, "Stand up straight, Archer. Let me get a good look at you." As he did, she was amazed at how different he looked than his older brothers. Where Matthew and Cameron were both dark-haired, Archer was a dusty blond, and even though he was tall like his brothers, at eighteen, his body hadn't yet filled out, leaving him looking tiny in comparison. But then, as Hattie took a closer look at his glittery smile and very handsome face, she knew without a doubt she was looking at a Forsythe.

"Is everything okay, Miss Hattie?" Archer asked unsure if he was living up to Hattie's expectations.

"Everything is fine," Hattie responded kindly. "I just like to get a good look at the people I'm entrusting my life too, and I must say that you are a fine looking young man. I am extremely happy to have you join my team of bodyguards, but then again, you did come highly recommended." Giving him a wink, she concluded, "I have a feeling we're going to end up great friends just like your brothers and I are."

Hardly able to contain his excitement, Archer impulsively threw his hands around Hattie, embracing her. Then, realizing what he was doing, he quickly moved away and apologized.

"For God's sake, Archer, you don't have to apologize," Hattie said sweetly as she straightened out her dress.

"You're not mad?" Archer responded with a blush.

"Not at all. I think it's wonderful that you're so happy. The world would be a much better place if we could all be as spontaneous and sweet as you just were. More importantly, though, you shouldn't feel like you have to apologize for doing what is in your heart. Emotions were meant to be expressed, not stifled. Okay?"

"Yes, Ma'am."

"All right, now, let's get you back to the mansion and start putting some meat on those bones. By this time next year, I want to see you as big as your brothers. I know you have the talent and brains to handle the job, but you need to work on your braun if you want to be my bodyguard."

Understanding perfectly, Archer nodded his head and graciously followed behind Hattie and his brothers to the carriage. Glancing skyward, he couldn't help but thank his lucky stars, and as he sat down inside of the carriage next to his two older brothers, he knew he was exactly where he was supposed to be.

***

LYING SILENT ON HIS BED, Ira's mind was racing. He hadn't been able to get his thoughts off of Nick Starr all day, and Walker's visit, as nice as it was, had only offered him temporary solace. Now, as the blackness of night enveloped his tiny prison cell like a shroud, his memories were driving him crazy. "All those months in the beginning when I thought Nick loved me," he thought to himself, "it was all lies." Getting to his feet, Ira paced the floor like a caged lion. "Damn him," he screamed in his mind. "I never wanted to hurt anybody, yet he made me believe it was the right thing to do. God, how could I have been such a fool?"

Walking to the window, Ira could see it was beginning to rain. "If Nick had just left me alone in the Dakotas, I could still have had a life, but instead, he had to drag me back into this mess. A mess which I told him repeatedly I wanted no part of. Yet, he never listened. He had to have his way, and now, nearly a year after his death, I'm the one paying the price." His thoughts were interrupted by a loud clap of thunder, and looking out of the window, he could see the rain was now coming down quite hard. Reaching up, Ira grabbed hold of the bars on the tiny window. "These bars of iron couldn't possibly imprison me any more than the ones in my mind." Returning to his bed, the thunder rolled rhythmically, shaking the walls of his cramped jail cell, while the flashes of lightning brought temporary light into Ira's dark world. Sitting there alone, Ira remembered nights just like these when he was a boy. More than once he had jumped from his own bed and ran to his father. Oh, how he missed his father now.

Sitting down on his bed and placing his head in his hands, Ira tried to deal with the sorrow he was feeling, but nothing, it seemed, could ease his pain. His thoughts continued to dwell on Nick and when they first met. Things were so different then. Nick would spend hours talking to him, sharing stories about the places he had been and the things he had done. Ira remembered how impressionable he was back then and how mesmerized he was by Nick. So much so that he was willing to do anything Nick wanted just to be near him. That, of course, Ira knew now was exactly what Nick had counted on, and within no time at all, the two of them were inseparable.

Ira knew Nick had worked hard to groom him, and it had taken months of hard work on his own part, as he learned how to conduct himself in higher social circles. Eventually and very intentionally, Nick created a gentleman of Ira. Following in Nick's footsteps, Ira wanted more than anything for Nick to be proud of him, and it was his insecurity that got him into trouble. He knew that Nick's intentions were wrong, but because he was so caught up in wanting to make Nick happy, he allowed himself to get talked into doing anything that Nick wanted. What the investigators had found out about Nick's real intention for Ira was true. He wanted to marry Ira off, not once but several times, to wealthy young women. In doing so, Nick could gain control of one fortune after another, making him and Ira wealthy beyond their wildest dreams.

That, at least, was the plan, but now, as Ira sat all alone in his cold jail cell, he realized his friendship and relationship with Nick had, without a doubt, ruined his life. What Ira once believed to be gold he could hold in his hands had now turned to dust and had slipped through his fingers.

Leaning backward on his bed until his head lay up against the damp stone wall, Ira closed his eyes and prayed to God for forgiveness for screwing up a life that had started out so promising, yet now, because of the choices he had made, lay in ruins at his feet.

***

SEVERAL HOURS LATER, Ira awoke to the sound of someone entering the jail. Stumbling to his feet, he wondered, "Who in the world could that be?" Walking to the entrance of his cell, he was surprised to see Mary Walsh talking with the Sheriff.

"You have a visitor, Ira," the Sheriff said loudly. Walking to Ira's cell, he opened it, and after letting Mary inside, he returned to his desk by the door.

Sitting back on his bed, Ira was baffled. "What are you doing here, Mary?"

"I be needin' to talk to you, Lad," she told him, as she took her cape off. It was still raining outside but not nearly as heavy as earlier.

"It's kind of late for you to be out by yourself," he replied nervously. "Is Hattie okay?"

"She be a doin' fine, Ira. She, Matthew, and the rest of the family be busy fussin' over Matthew's brother, Archer, who just be arrivin' from Salt Lake. That be why I be choosin' tonight to be sneakin' out and comin' to talk with you, because I be knowin' that everybody would be stayin' busy."

Nodding his head, Ira leaned forward and asked, "If it's not Hattie you've come to talk to me about, what is it then?"

"It be a lot of thin's actually, but mainly, I be worried a lot about Miss Dakota."

Sitting straight up, Ira's heart raced. "What about her, Mary? She isn't starting to . . .?" His voice trailed off as he looked into Mary's eyes intently.

"Be rememberin' what happened that night? No, it not be nothin' like that. At least, not that I be knowin' about. But, I do have me concerns." Starting to cry, Mary reached out and took his hand. "You just don't be deservin' this, Lad."

Quickly getting to his feet, he embraced Mary and led her to an old wooden chair in the corner of his cell. Kneeling down in front of her and stroking her hand compassionately, he wiped the tears from her eyes. "Look, Mary, you know how this has to be. We've talked about it before. I'm depending on you to be strong."

"Me know, Lad. Me know. It just be so hard knowin' the truth, and there not be a thin' I can be doin' about it."

"You're right, Mary, it is hard. It's very hard, but neither you nor Dakota nor anyone else is responsible for what happened that night. I've spent all day thinking about this, and it is painfully clear that I got myself into this mess a long time ago. I tried to break free of Nick, Lord knows I tried, but it was too late."

"But you be so young, Lad, and most likely by the New Year you be dead."

"Unless a miracle happens, it's looking more and more that way. I wish it could be different, I really do, but given the circumstances, it just can't be any other way."

"So what be happenin' next?"

"Nothing, Mary. Nothing happens next. I'm going to be a man and take whatever punishment the Judge decides to give me. Whatever it is, Mary, I deserve it, and to be honest with you, nothing the Judge sentences me to could possibly be any worse than the mental anguish that I've been going through as of late. I have not lived a good life by any stretch of the imagination, and if being hanged is what the Judge orders, then that is my debt to pay. But as God as my witness, I'm not going to let one fateful encounter ruin so many lives."

Chapter 3
THE POWER OF LOVE

IN THE DAYS LEADING UP to the Judge's six month deadline, Robert and John, in an effort to offer moral support to the family, both moved back to the mansion until things smoothed out where Ira was concerned. Hattie was extremely happy to have her entire family around her again, but yet, at the same time, it was a very bittersweet reunion, as she knew that Ira's imminent sentencing and subsequent death was what was bringing them together.

With the day of the hearing finally upon them, Hattie dressed up in one of her most beautiful blue sapphire dresses. "I may not be able to do anything about Ira's situation," she told her mother, as she stood in front of her full length mirror and readied herself for the big day, "but one thing that I do have control over is how I look. And for Ira's sake, I want to look my absolute best."

Listening intently, Minerva couldn't keep herself from tearing up. "I am so proud of you."

Turning to see her mother's tears, Hattie gently wiped them away. "Why on earth are you crying?" she asked confused.

"Even now, after all this time and all the heartache that you've been through, you're only thought is to look good for your husband. Honestly, Hattie, your selflessness amazes me."

"Don't get me wrong, Mother," Hattie responded softly yet firmly,

"I always want to look good. I believe that it is a person's duty to always present themselves well, no matter what the occasion, but in this case, yes, I must admit I'm thinking of Ira. Most likely after today the only thing Ira is going to have to look forward too is a date with the gallows, and personally, I want to do everything in my power to make his last days, good days."

Hearing Hattie's strong words, Minerva couldn't help but beam with pride. Some people who take marriage vows don't really mean it and run at the first sign of trouble. Hattie, on the other hand, despite her young age and relative inexperience, was a firm believer in 'till death do us part', and she was not about to abandon Ira just because the going got a little tough. Watching Hattie return to her mirror and finish getting ready, Minerva again marveled at her daughter's exceptional class and grace. "This angel of a woman," she thought gratefully, "is my daughter. How in the world did I get so lucky?" It was a question that Minerva had asked herself many times before over the years, yet now, more than ever, a sufficient answer escaped her.

***

ABOUT AN HOUR LATER, Hattie sat bundled up in her carriage as Cameron and Matthew went over final preparations for their trip to the courthouse. The temperate, autumn weather that they had been having only weeks before had now turned to full-fledged winter, and Hattie could see snowflakes cascading down from the heavens outside of her carriage windows. It was times like these that she thanked God for being able to travel in the relative comfort of the enclosed carriages rather than the open buggies that were more fit for summertime. Waiting patiently, Hattie could hear Matthew giving instructions to her men outside in the cold.

"Archer, you take the reins and drive Miss Hattie's carriage. John,

Robert, Shannon, and I will ride with you while George will drive Minerva, James, Dakota, and Ira's family in the other carriage. The rest of you surround the carriages tightly on horseback." Shaking his head while shivering slightly, Matthew's tone grew very serious. "For some reason, I've got a bad feeling about today, Men. I want all of you to be on extra high alert."

Within minutes everyone else was in their respective carriages, and Archer led them through the snow on their way to Gallatin.

Scooting up next to Hattie, Robert gave her a peck on the cheek and covered her up with another blanket. "Better keep warm, Sis, it's cold out there."

Looking around at her three loving brothers, Hattie asked, "What have I ever done to deserve brothers as wonderful as you?"

Laughing, Robert rolled his eyes. "I think, Hattie, that you've got this all wrong. It would be more correct to say, 'What did we ever do to deserve you?'."

In spite of the serious purpose of their trip that morning, the ride to the courthouse was surprisingly pleasant. They spent their time talking about the fact that John and Robert had left Robert's ranch in Caldwell County to return to Silver Creek. Even though Hattie had sent several telegrams saying that she would be fine, they insisted they be with the rest of the family during these trying times. Like they had always done in the past, the Morran family came together in support of each other, and in doing so, they were able to overcome life's challenges. Robert, knowing of Hattie's concern, assured her that the ranch was in good hands and that he and his wife Amanda, as well as John and Shannon, felt their place was at her side.

"We wouldn't miss a chance to help for the world," John reassured her kindly.

"I must admit," Hattie said honestly, "I feel much better with everyone here with me. I just wish that Lou and Rebecca could be here as well."

"Have you heard from them lately?" Robert asked, curious.

"Yes," Hattie responded. "They are still in Richmond, but I think that after today, no matter what the outcome of the hearing is, I am going to telegram and ask them to return for Christmas. They have been gone far too long, and I miss their company. It would be wrong in my opinion to allow these unfounded death threats to ruin our holidays. What do you think?" Looking at her brothers, they nodded their heads in agreement, but Matthew, who sat quietly in the corner of the carriage, couldn't help but worry. Death threats were now arriving almost daily at Silver Creek against Hattie, Lou, and anyone connected with them. Matthew thought it was sad indeed that with all Hattie and Lou's wealth, they were forced to live under such heavily guarded conditions and alter their lives just to have peace of mind. Leaning his head against the wall of the carriage, he desperately hoped that the uneasy feelings he was having were just nerves, but at the same time, he couldn't help but fear they were much more.

Reaching the courthouse, James, Hattie, and Matthew went immediately to see Ira, while the rest of the family and Hattie's men took their seats in the courtroom. Approaching the small room where Ira was being held before the hearing, Hattie could see Sheriff Sanders guarding the door. After exchanging greetings, Hattie and James quickly entered the room, while Matthew stood patiently outside with the Sheriff.

"Aren't you going to go in too, Matt?"

"No, Sheriff, not this time. James has some pretty important things to go over with Ira, and after he's done with that, I feel that Ira and Hattie deserve some privacy."

Nodding his head, the Sheriff took a deep breath. "You know, Matt, I don't think I've ever told you how much respect I have for you and your men. Your desire to help Ira and Miss Hattie is nothing short of amazing. It's a rare thing in this day and age to see such selflessness and devotion. Most people are just out to get everything they can in life, but as far as I've seen, you and your men are just the opposite. Miss Hattie's lucky to have you."

"Thank you, Sheriff. It's very kind of you to say that."

"I mean it. You and your men are top notch citizens in my book. You could be a very stabilizing influence in this community, if you ever decided to settle down here."

"I highly doubt it, Sheriff," Matthew replied with a smile. "Our home is in the top of the Rocky Mountains with our families, but you're right about one thing. We're all very much devoted to Hattie."

"I see that, and I can understand why. I've known her since she was knee-high to a grasshopper, and she has always been loved by most everyone who has ever known her. She has a heart of gold, and all that money hasn't changed her one bit. I've watched her as she's become a real lady, and regardless of her wealth or position in life, I believe she'll always be the same sweet country girl she's always been."

Inside the room, James, Hattie, and Ira were sitting around a small wooden table. The small size of the room and the barren windowless walls only accentuated the feeling of despair that Ira was feeling inside his soul. Staring blankly ahead, Ira listened silently as James gave him the blunt facts concerning the hearing. He explained how, with no new evidence, the Judge would surely sentence him to hang and also that there would be no more second chances. Reaching the end of the discussion, James said solemnly, "Ira, as much as I hate to admit it, we've reached the end of our road. I really wish things could have worked out, but it was just not to be." Struggling with his emotions, he said, "I'm sorry that I was not able to find any evidence to clear you. I really thought six months ago that we could find something, but in the end, we came up short."

Moving for the first time since James and Hattie had entered the room, Ira reached up and touched James's arm. "It's not your fault, James. You did everything you could. Promise me that you'll never hang your head when you think about me or this case." Getting no response, Ira repeated himself. "I mean it, James, promise me." Seeing James nod in the affirmative, Ira continued. "You are a damn good lawyer, James. You're a good husband, a great father, and an excellent friend, which is much more than can be said about me." Extending his hand, he shook James's. "Thank you for all that you've done. You've given me more than I ever could have hoped for, especially with the way I treated you in the beginning. So please, after today, don't worry about me. I'll be fine. Now, if you don't mind, I would like to talk to Hattie privately."

Nodding again, James got to his feet and gave Ira a final pat on the shoulder before making his way to the door. As he exited, Ira sighed heavily. Without looking at Hattie, he spoke somberly. "I sincerely hope that marrying me hasn't destroyed your life."

"Destroyed my life?" she replied quickly. "Not a chance, Ira. If anything, you've enriched it. I know that may be hard to believe, as horrible as it has been at times, but I've learned a lot from this experience. Standing by you through this mess has taught me just how precious life can be. I decided long ago when I married Abner Garland that if I'm going to go through this life just once, I'm not going to let anyone or anything destroy me."

Unable to control his emotions anymore, tears welled up in Ira's eyes. He had been trying so hard to stay composed and did a good job while talking with James, but hearing Hattie's kind and compassionate words, Ira couldn't pretend any longer. His sorrow was tearing him up inside, and as the tears flowed freely down his face, he stammered, "But I treated you so horrible, and I failed you in so many ways. Can you ever forgive me for what I have done?"

Reaching across the tiny table, Hattie gently wiped away the stream of tears from his cheek. "I already have, Ira," she replied compassionately. "I admit that in the beginning I was very frustrated with things, and I didn't understand why you acted and still act so withdrawn from me. But don't ever confuse that frustration with forgiveness, because you were forgiven long ago."

"I don't know why," Ira responded, bewildered. "I don't deserve it."

"It's not a matter of whether you deserve it or not, Ira. I've lived long enough to know that it is better to forgive than to hold a grudge. Grudges only cause heartache and pain, and personally, I have seen enough heartache and pain. Besides, it really isn't my place to judge anyway. That is the Almighty's job. He and He alone knows why you've done the things you've done. He's the one you need to make peace with, not me."

Closing his eyes tightly, Ira knew Hattie was right. "I've been trying to make peace with Him, I really have, but I can't help but think that it's too late."

"Well, I don't know if it can ever be too late to repent for that which you have done, but I will tell you this. As long as it comes from the depths of your soul, a late repentance is better than no repentance at all, and I, for one, wouldn't waste one minute I had left. If you're really worried about your place in the hereafter, I wouldn't stop praying for a second. I know that I've never stopped praying for you," she said solemnly, as tears began to well up in her own eyes.

Scooting her chair over to Ira, she embraced him tenderly, and together they cried for several minutes. They cried over the past, they cried over the present situation they found themselves in, and they cried over a future that they would never see together. Most of all, they cried to release the pain of a year's worth of sorrows. All the months and months of pent up emotions poured out all at once, and after they finished, they both felt better than they had in a long time. Their peace was short-lived, though, as the Sheriff knocked loudly and then entered the room.

"It's time, Ira," he said firmly. "The Judge is just about ready."

After embracing Hattie one final time, Ira rose to his feet and followed the Sheriff out of the tiny room. As the Sheriff led Ira into courtroom, Hattie and Matthew hurried to get to their seats.

With everyone finally ready, Judge Stepp made his entrance and slowly took his seat. Looking out over his bench and down at James, his tone was deadly serious. "Well, Mr. Kinnion, here we are. It's November 20th, and you have had over six months to conduct your detailed investigation. Tell me, what were your findings?"

Standing up, James's demeanor was humble yet strong, and even though he was visibly disappointed, he spoke confidently and firmly. "Despite our best efforts, Your Honor, we were unable to find anything that would make a difference in this case."

Sensing James's disappointment, the Judge leaned forward in his chair. "I heard all about Newton, James. I know that you had hoped to get answers from him, but the funny thing about life is that things seldom go as you plan and never as you hope. I am truly sorry that things didn't work out better than they did, but you understand my position and what I must do now. I feared this would be the case six months ago. That is why I was slow to agree to your request, but now, I've done all that I can do." Turning to Ira, the Judge cleared his throat. "Do you understand what this means, Ira?"

"Yes."

"Then, with my deepest condolences, I assign December 28th, 1899 as your day of execution by hanging. May God have mercy on your soul."

***

WITH THE HEARING OVER, the Sheriff immediately went to take Ira back to the jail. With the Sheriff's permission, Hattie accompanied Ira in the Sheriff's buggy on their way to the jail, while Hattie's men and her older brothers followed closely behind with her carriage. Knowing they could do nothing more, James and the rest of the family went home feeling devastated. Even though everyone had known in their hearts what the Judge was going to say, the finality of knowing that by the New Year Ira would be gone was hard to accept. Ira's sisters took the final sentencing the hardest, hardly able to stop crying all the way home.

Making the short trip to the jail through the freshly fallen snow, Hattie tried to offer Ira encouragement, but it was to no avail. He seemed lost in the depths of his own mind, and knowing what his fate was, Hattie didn't blame him. Sitting silent, she simply tried to be of some comfort, but deep down, she feared that their stolen moment of closeness in the courthouse would be their last together, as Ira seemed to drift further and further down the lonely road of despair.

Arriving at the jail, Hattie walked Ira to his cell, embraced him a final time, and said her final goodbyes. Meeting Matthew just inside the entrance of the jail, she was visibly distraught.

"I know you feel helpless in dealing with Ira, Hattie," Matthew said kindly, "but trust in God. Somehow, even when things look hopeless, the power of His love makes things right."

Hearing Matthew's kind words, Hattie felt a strange feeling come over her. Exiting the jail, she gazed out at the snow-covered wonderland with a sense of urgency. "Something is about to happen," she told herself, as she watched Archer pull the carriage up to jail's steps. With the snow now quite deep, Archer got as close as he could, but just as Hattie was stepping into the carriage, her foot slipped and he lunged across the seat in an effort to grab her arm. As she fell to her knee, a rifle shot rang out from an alley across the street, striking Archer in the shoulder. Slumping forward in his seat, the reins on the carriage pulled backward causing the horses to bolt forward several feet, exposing Hattie to the open street. Acting quickly, Matthew grabbed Hattie, held her tightly in his arms, and turned his back to the street, shielding her with his body. Second and third shots were fired almost instantaneously, finding their mark in Matthew's back and causing him to slump forward on top of Hattie, knocking her to the ground. In the distance, Hattie could hear women screaming before suddenly feeling the weight of a second and third body covering both her and Matthew. The rest of Hattie's men immediately ran and fired in the direction of the shots, but it was too late, as a man on horseback rode off down the alley across the street at full gallop.

Cameron and Hattie's brother John, getting to their feet, realized when they saw the blood on the back of Matthew's coat that he had taken the bullets meant for Hattie. Seeing blood across the front of Hattie's dress and cape, Cameron thought she had been shot, too. Hattie, seeing the look on his face, quickly assured him, "I'm fine, Cameron, I'm just shook up."

"I'm sorry, Miss Hattie, we weren't expecting this," he said, discouraged.

"Neither was I, but don't blame yourselves, you did everything you could." Looking into the faces of her men, she reassured, "all of you did." As Matthew lay unconscious in the arms of several men, Jack Forsythe carefully pulled Archer out of the carriage and sat him down on the steps of the jail. Hattie then sent two of her other bodyguards, Joseph Taylor and his brother Brigham for Doc Cowley, whose office was down the street. Having heard the gunfire, the kindly old Doctor was already headed in their direction, meeting them halfway. Upon examining Archer, he found that he had taken a bullet to the shoulder, but it wasn't life threatening. Matthew, on the other hand, had taken both bullets meant for Hattie, and one, it appeared, was very close to his heart. Seeing this, the doctor was emphatic. "We've got to move Matthew into the jail, Boys, as quickly and as carefully as possible."

Cameron, filled with incredible grief, turned to Hattie and pleaded. "Please, Miss Hattie, let us give him a blessing before he's moved."

Hattie, knowing how important their faith was to them, readily agreed. "By all means, Cameron."

"Miss Hattie, we don't have time for this," the Doctor insisted.

"Oh, yes we do, Doc. We do, and we will. I've grown to love Matthew as much as I love anybody in this world, and if Cameron says a blessing will help him, by God he's going to get one."

Cameron and Joseph knelt next to Matthew, as the other men formed a private circle around them. As they began, townspeople began to gather all about, talking loudly and causing a distraction. Brigham pleaded with them to be quiet, so they could pray for their friend, but it seemed that the people in the crowd just got louder. Stepping outside the circle, Hattie was furious. Yelling above the noise of the crowd, she glared at the noisy onlookers. "All right, you people, I don't want to hear another peep out of anybody until these men are finished." A hush quickly fell over the crowd, as they recognized Hattie, and no one dared mess with her. Stepping back inside the circle of safety, Hattie said, "Go ahead, Cameron."

After placing a small amount of anointed oil on Matthew's head, Cameron began praying. His deep clear voice rang out through the still falling snow like thunder, and by the time he finished there wasn't a dry eye anywhere to be found. Even Doc Cowley couldn't help but feel better about Matthew's chances after hearing Cameron pour out his soul to the Almighty.

Getting to his feet, Cameron and several of the other men reached beneath their fallen brother and carefully cradled his unconscious body in their arms. Others surrounded Hattie, shielding her and Matthew, as they moved him into the jail. Inside they found a deputy had cleared a large table in the corner of the room, and gently, the men laid Matthew on it.

Ira was horrified when he saw Hattie's dress and cape covered in blood. The Sheriff, understanding Ira's concern, bolted the jailhouse door from the inside and released him from his cell.

Racing to Hattie, he embraced her. "I'm okay," she reassured him. "It's Matthew that we need to worry about." Turning to Wesley Pitcock and Randy Brown, two more of her bodyguards, she insisted they return to the estate and inform the rest of the family about what had happened. "Tell them that I'm fine, and have them meet us here at the jail as soon as the weather will permit." As they hurried for the door and Hattie took off her soiled cape, the Sheriff asked if she wouldn't rather return with Randy and Wesley to Silver Creek for her own safety.

"Heavens, no!" she replied emphatically. "I'm staying right here with Matthew. My place is with my men, and I'll not leave his side until I know he is out of danger." Turning to Ira, she asked, "You understand, don't you Ira? You know how much I love him."

Managing a small smile, Ira said, "Of course I understand, Hattie. I care for him, too. He's been like a brother to me."

Starting to work on Matthew's wounds, the Doctor called out to Hattie. "I'm going to need you, Miss Hattie. Will you help me?"

Without a second thought, she hurriedly pushed up her sleeves. "Of course, Doc, what can I do?"

"I wouldn't have asked, but I remember how well you helped me when Shannon was shot in the leg. There was a lot of blood involved that day, but you didn't flinch. Do you think you can handle this?"

"Believe me, I can handle anything if it will help in saving Matthew."

Standing silent, Cameron continued to pray as he watched the Doctor working to save his brother's life. Several other men held coal oil lamps and watched anxiously as Hattie helped the doctor. There was such a loss of blood that Matthew grew as pale as a ghost. At first Hattie felt sick, but she never flinched, especially when Matthew came to then passed out again from the pain. The doctor had been right. Helping him when Shannon was accidentally shot in the leg was nothing compared to Matthew's extensive injuries. She shuttered as she watched the expressions on the Doctor's face grow more and more grim. They told her that he wasn't sure if Matthew was going to make it.

Pausing momentarily, Doc Cowley looked up and said, "Miss Hattie, please send one of your boys for some whiskey."

"You're not planning to give him whiskey for the pain, are you, Doc?"

"Yes, and to cleanse the wound. Trust me, after this is over, he's going to need something pretty bad. The pain is going to be excruciating."

"I can't let you give him whiskey, Doc," Hattie replied earnestly. "Matthew told me that he's never tasted liquor. His wound is one thing, but having to drink the liquor is quite another. These men are Mormons, you know they don't drink."

"That's all well and good, Miss Hattie, but you have no idea how great the pain will be. I've got very little to give him other than whiskey."

"He'll be okay," she reassured him. "You heard his brother bless him that the pain would be minimal."

"Yes, Miss Hattie, and I'm a religious man, but . . ."

"Then, have faith, Doc, that he'll be able to endure the pain. Whatever it is about their religion and this special Priesthood power they hold, it gives them tremendous faith and spiritual strength."

"And why, may I ask, do you believe that?"

"I've seen their faith in action, that's why, and if these men say they can do something, believe me, they can!"

"Better watch it, Miss Hattie, sounds like these men have just about got you converted."

Hattie smiled. "Not hardly, Doc, but I do respect them for their beliefs."

Returning to Matthew's wounds, the Doctor found the first bullet and extracted it. Using some of the whiskey he had on hand, he cleansed the wound. Then, with great beads of perspiration running down his face, he said quietly, "Now for the really difficult one." A few minutes later, the doctor had removed the second bullet. He cleansed the wound, sewed it closed, and carefully bandaged it.

"Is he going to pull through?" Hattie asked anxiously.

"Only time will tell," the Doctor replied unsure. "Things look good so far, but with the location of that second bullet so close to his heart, it will be difficult to tell for awhile. All we can do is wait patiently and hope for the best."

Cleaning her hands, Hattie was exhausted. As she returned to

Matthew's side, Cameron got her a chair and placed it close enough to Matthew so she could lay her head on his arm.

Leaving them alone for a moment, Cameron watched as Doc Cowley finished taking care of Archer's flesh wound. One of the men had taken care of it earlier, but the Doctor wanted to check it over himself. Once he finished, Archer and Cameron took their places next to Hattie.

For the next two hours, Ira stood behind Hattie with his hands on her shoulders patiently waiting for any sign of life from Matthew. Finally growing weary, she stood, and together, she and Ira walked to his cell. As she sat on his bed, he knelt on one knee next to her, holding her hand. "I'll never be able to thank Matthew enough for saving your life."

"Neither will I, but I'm sure going to try. Whatever he or Archer want or need, I'll see that they have it, Ira."

"I know I wasn't very responsive on our way back from the courthouse today, Hattie. I know that you only want to help me, but some things I just have to work out on my own. Do you understand?"

Taking a deep breath, Hattie brushed Ira's wavy brown hair away from his eyes. "You know what, Ira, for the first time I think I do. I didn't used to, that's for sure. I thought that you didn't trust me, that you didn't care."

"Oh, Hattie," Ira interjected, "that was never the case."

"I know that now," Hattie responded weakly. "Matthew has helped me greatly in trying to understand you over the past year. His good counsel is the main reason why I'm able to deal with things so much better than I have previously."

"Believe me Hattie, I would've given anything if things could have turned out differently, but they just didn't. I realize that you have many questions, but with the circumstances the way they are, there's no way

I could tell you things. And unfortunately, I still can't." Placing his finger over her lips as she started to ask why, he continued. "I know that this is hard for you to accept, but it is the way it has to be. Please just know that I never wanted to hurt you, and it is because I still don't want to hurt you that I must remain silent. It is the very best for everyone that it be this way." Smiling weakly, he sat next to her on the bed and put his arm around her. "Please don't take this wrong, Hattie, but when I'm gone," he paused, trying to find the right words, "Matt is the kind of man that I would like for you to marry."

Hattie looked at him in disbelief. "Why, don't be silly, Ira. Why in the world would you even say such a thing? He's a Mormon. He'll not marry a woman unless she is a member of his faith. Why on earth are you concerning yourself about something like that at a time like this?"

"I don't think it's odd for me to be concerned about you. I'm your husband, and I care about you. I'm just facing facts, Hattie."

"Loving Matthew, Ira, is not the same thing as being in love with him and you know it."

"For once in your life, Hattie Saxon, don't be so damn stubborn. I see the way you two look at each other, and if one day in the future the opportunity should arise, for heaven's sake, don't be so foolish as to brush Matt aside."

Biting her lip nervously, Hattie knew Ira was right, but realizing how difficult a relationship would be with Matthew, she was afraid of having too deep of feelings for him. Placing the thought of it out of her mind, she said, "I'm sorry, Ira, but right now all I care about is that he lives."

As the hours continued to pass with no change, Hattie began to get very worried, not only about Matthew but also about her family. "They should have made it back here by now," she thought nervously. Pacing from one side of the jail to the other, she was relieved when Randy and Wesley finally returned with James, Dakota, and Minerva. "Thank God you made it," she told them, as she embraced them one by one. "Between the three of you and Matthew, I was worrying myself sick."

"We hurried as fast as we could," Minerva replied breathless, "but the weather is absolutely frightful out there. Once we got home earlier, the winds really picked up out in the country, and they only just let up enough so that we could make it into town again. It is absolutely amazing to me that Randy and Wesley were able to make it out to Silver Creek in such blizzard-like conditions."

Calling out above their conversation, Doc Cowley could hardly contain his excitement. "He's waking up!"

Gathering around the table, everyone watched anxiously as Matthew moaned and then finally opened his eyes.

Looking out at the sea of people around him, Matthew one by one recognized the Doctor, his brothers, his companions, and Hattie and her family standing around him. "What's going on?" he asked weakly. "Did I die, or what?"

Doc Cowley smiled and assured him, "No, Son, you didn't die. But you couldn't have gotten any closer to it than you did."

As Hattie tenderly took Matthew's hand in her own, tears welled up in her eyes. Bending forward, she moved to kiss Matthew but stopped. Looking up, she saw Ira approach from his cell. It was obvious she wanted his approval, and feeling under the circumstances it was indeed the right thing, he nodded. Bending down again, she kissed Matthew tenderly on the lips and gently brushed his hair away from his forehead. "Matthew, you crazy Elder, you nearly got yourself killed over me."

Weakly, Matthew forced himself to speak. As the words fell

painfully from his lips, his eyes filled with tears. "If you recall . . . Hattie
. . . that's what . . . I'm paid to do."

"No, no, no, Matthew. You're hired to protect me, not die for me."
Looking around at each of her men, she said, "I don't know how I'd
live with myself if one of you died for me."

"With as serious as his wounds were, Hattie, how could he have escaped death?" Dakota asked, amazed.

Remembering Matthew's last words before the shooting, Hattie
replied, "It was by the 'power of love', Cody. All of us in this room
were praying for him, and God heard our prayers."

Chapter 4
IN THE HANDS OF ANGELS

IN THE DAYS AFTER THE SHOOTING, Matthew recovered at an amazing pace, and after only a few weeks, he was nearly back to normal. Visiting with Hattie and Minerva in the parlor, he walked slowly from the fireplace and sat down on a chair near the window.

Walking to his side, Hattie was brimming with happiness over his speedy recovery. Wrapping her arms around his neck, she kissed his head softly and said, "I'm so thankful that you're okay. I honestly don't know what I would have done, if you hadn't made it."

Smiling weakly, Matthew spoke kindly yet honestly. "You would have gone on, Hattie. You see, that's the one truth about life. No matter what happens, it goes on."

"That it does, Matthew. But at the same time, I'm not going to let the miracle that allowed you to live go unnoticed or unappreciated. One of the biggest problems in this world is that people don't appreciate what they have. And I don't ever want to let that happen to me, because it's as the old adage says, 'That which you don't appreciate, God will take away from you'."

"Hattie," Minerva said softly, "I don't mean to interrupt, but did you ever hear back from Lou and Rebecca. It has been awhile since you contacted them, and I want to know if we should be expecting them for Christmas."

"I just received a telegram today," Hattie replied excited, "that said they will be arriving on the 15th."

"What else did they say?" Minerva asked, curious.

Breathing deeply, Hattie thought back to the telegram. "Just how excited they were to finally be coming home and how sorry they were that they weren't here to offer moral support after Matthew and Archer were shot."

"They aren't worried about their own safety?"

"It's not that they're not worried, Mother," Hattie replied matter-of-factly, "but it's like I've said before. I can't live my life being scared all the time of what might happen, and they feel the same way." Pausing, she sighed heavily. "I'd give anything if I could guarantee our safety, but I can't. No one can. We have taken every possible precaution that we can take, and the incident at the jail notwithstanding, I feel that we are well equipped to deal with anything that will come up. Beyond that, we're 'in the hands of angels'."

As their conversation fell silent, the only sounds that could be heard were the ticking of the grandfather clock and a shutter outside the window banging in the wind. Surveying the parlor, Hattie never ceased to be amazed at the beauty around her. The ornate woodwork and craftsmanship that had gone into the mansion construction was absolutely fabulous in her eyes, and in silence she again thanked God for her many blessings in life.

Making her way to the window, Hattie gazed out at the winter landscape. The snow seemed to sparkle in the sunlight, and the green of the evergreen trees added just the right amount of color. To Hattie, it looked more like a painting than a view out of a window, but then, when a deer ran across the snow in the distance, she was reminded it wasn't."

As she stood motionless in front of the window, her silhouette could be seen for some distance. In a grove of trees not far from the mansion, a lone figure raised a rifle, taking Hattie in its sight. Suddenly, without warning, the heavy drapes on the window were yanked shut obstructing the man's view. Furious, he threw his rifle to the ground. "Damn! Damn! Damn!" he muttered under his breath. "How can that woman be so lucky?"

The drapes shut so quickly, that it startled not only Hattie but Matthew and Minerva as well. Searching for an explanation, they found Mary by the window holding the drawing cords with a disgusted expression on her face. "What be wrong with you, Lass? It be a very foolish thin', you standin' in front of this window after someone be tryin' to shoot you in Gallatin!"

Still not knowing how Mary had managed to walk up unnoticed, Hattie took a second to calm herself. "Now, Mary," Hattie replied softly, "we have men riding the fence lines day and night. Everything ought to be pretty safe here at home."

"Like they be the day of your weddin' when a bullet came sailin' through the doors and be a lodgin' itself into the wall?"

"Perhaps you're right," Hattie responded discouraged, as she remembered back to her wedding day. "Maybe I'm not safe anywhere."

Disgruntled, Mary walked out of the room mumbling and shaking her head.

Passing her in the doorway, James and Dakota entered the parlor and asked in unison, "What's wrong with Mary?"

"Oh, she's just worried about my standing in front of the window."

Dakota sighed. "You really can't blame her, Hattie. She loves you so much, and she's only looking out for your best interest. To tell you the truth, I think all of us in this family lack a little when it comes to good old common sense. Thank goodness we have someone like Mary to remind us about things from time to time. Because, if that at the jail proved anything, it's that we can't be too safe.

***

LATER THAT WEEK, in an attempt to handle some of the final arrangements concerning Ira's hanging, Hattie and Matthew met with him at the jail. As the Sheriff let Hattie into his cell, she was pleasantly surprised to find that he was writing. Sitting down next to him, she said softly, "I see you took my advice and decided to write."

Putting his materials aside, Ira slowly nodded his head. "At first I wasn't going to, but after what happened to Matt, I felt compelled to at least give it try."

"That's wonderful, Ira," Hattie replied happily.

"The crazy thing is since I've started, I haven't been able to stop. I've been writing nonstop now for over two weeks, and though I'm still discouraged about a lot of things, I do feel better in a lot of ways." Giving Hattie a smile, Ira touched her hand tenderly. "Thank you, Hattie, for everything."

"Don't mention it," she said, as she gave him a quick peck on the cheek. Leaning back, Hattie's bright smile lit up the cold, dark jail cell.

With his voice turning serious, Ira said, "So, what's brought you here today?"

"We need to go over your final arrangements, Ira," Hattie replied solemnly. "We've avoided the subject far too long. I know it's a subject that we have gone out of our way to avoid numerous times, but we needn't add foolishness to everything else that has happened to us."

Agreeing, Ira listened as Hattie told him of her fears and plans.

An hour later, Hattie and Matthew left the jail and went directly to the Undertaker's to make arrangements for Ira's coffin. Her request was that it be lined in the same pale blue material as the dress and cape which she was planning to wear to the hanging.

As Matthew handed the material to the undertaker, he asked, "Can you do it, Mr. Scarborough?"

"Yes, Mr. Forsythe, I can, but I must admit, I've never had a request for a casket lining in this color."

Since Ira's hanging would be the first legal hanging ever held in Daviess County, Missouri, it was expected to be a big event. Leaving the Funeral Parlor, Hattie and Matthew walked to the telegraph office. There she wired the Sheriff at Princeton, requesting that he join forces with Sheriff Sanders and help in protecting Ira in case of unruly crowds the day of the hanging.

Finished with the tasks at hand, they made their way to a local hotel dining room for supper. Feeling that Hattie needed something to take her mind off of Ira, Minerva suggested that she, Matthew, James, and Dakota spend the night out. James and Dakota arrived as expected, but unfortunately, Laville was right behind them. She had bumped into James earlier in the day at the bank, and hearing of the family's evening plans, she insisted that she be invited. Entering the room in a beautiful black flowing gown, she was stunning as usual. Her date for the evening, however, left much to be desired. His name was Robert Holmes, a very wealthy but obnoxious farmer from Caldwell County. He only stood a mere four feet eleven inches tall and was as bald as an eagle. As if that wasn't already a winning combination, he was as over-bearing, proud, and as obstinate as he could possibly be to everyone but Laville. Taking his seat between Laville and Dakota, he showed his true colors from the very start.

As Hattie listened to him, it seemed to her as though Mr. Holmes couldn't make enough sarcastic remarks and innuendos about Mormons. Everyone, especially Matthew and Hattie's men did their best to ignore his ignorant statements, yet, as Laville rudely burst out in laughter after every remark, Dakota Jayne became more and more angry by the minute. James, seeing the exasperated look crossing her face, knew she was about to explode. Mr. Holmes's rudeness finally reached its peak when his remarks were turned directly toward Matthew.

"And you, Pretty Boy, how many wives do you have, four, five, six perhaps?"

"Actually, Mr. Holmes, I'm not married."

"Oh, you're not, huh? What's the matter, can't find a girl as pretty as yourself?"

As Laville again rudely burst into laughter, Dakota threw her napkin on her plate in disgust. Shoving her chair back so hard it tipped over, she stood angrily with her hands on her hips. With all eyes upon her, her raised voice reverberated around the dining hall. "Mr. Holmes, I would think that a man of your means would have some sophistication and at least a teeny weeny bit of tact, but after listening to you run that rat trap you call a mouth for the last half hour, it is obvious that you don't! You may think poking fun at others is a real hoot, but in my book, it only proves how stupid and ignorant you really are. Considering such, it makes what I am about to do just that much easier." Reaching over, she dumped his hot plate of food into his lap, picked up the fresh pie that she knew had been placed in front of her, and dumped it on top of his head.

Laville screamed, "Dakota, what in the hell has come over you?"

"A sense of decency, I hope! What in the hell has come over you, Laville? How can you sit there and let this idiot make fun of the very men who have cared so much for you and have protected you with their very lives?"

"But . . . but . . . ," Laville protested.

"Shut up, Laville! I don't want to hear it! Your sanctioning the bab-
blings of this horse's ass has brought utter disgrace to our family. Now,
please get out of here, and take this damn leprechaun with you!" Complete silence fell over the dining room. Then, one by one, the people
began to clap their hands. They started slowly at first, but soon they
clapped louder and louder until finally several men in the room were
whistling. Hurrying from the table, Laville left with Mr. Holmes, who
never again showed his face in Gallatin.

Smiling proudly, Hattie said, "I couldn't have said it better, Sis."

***

THE FOLLOWING MONDAY, Rebecca and Lou arrived in Gallatin
as scheduled, and from the minute they stepped off the train, they were
eager to here all about the many events that had happened in their ab-
sence. Elated to finally have two of her dearest friends and confidants
back by her side, Hattie assured them that, even though the summer of
1899 was being referred to as the summer of love, she, personally, had
lived through the summer from hell.

Arriving at the mansion, everyone settled into the parlor to continue
their discussion, but before they could even get started, Sheriff Sanders
made a surprise visit, needing to talk with Hattie.

The family became very discouraged when they heard what the
Sheriff had to say, as he told them the very thing they had all feared.
"I'm sorry to have to tell you this, but I've been ordered by the Court
to have a large stockade built around the town square, where the gallows
are being constructed," he said solemnly.

Listening to the Sheriff's news, Hattie was disgusted. Until now,
this had only been a rumor, but as the realization of it hit home, Hattie
began to grow sick. Taking her mother's hand, she listened as the
Sheriff continued.

"Over seven hundred tickets are bein' issued to the townspeople, and though I've tried from the start to stop this from happenin', Stanley Johnson has convinced the Judge that the citizens of Gallatin have a right to view the hangin'.

Lou stood in disgust. "I can't believe this! How could a hanging have gone from a legal execution to a side show?"

Sheriff Sanders felt awful to have to deliver such devastating news to Hattie. Standing discouraged before her, he said sadly, "I only hope, Miss Hattie, that we can control the crowd. Because of your fore-thought in contacting the Sheriff over in Princeton, we have his total support and the use of his deputies for that day, but even with his help, controlling seven hundred ticket holders, not to mention the countless hundreds that are sure to congregate outside the enclosure, will be a monumental task."

Leaning forward in her chair, Hattie had a plan. After explaining herself to everyone, she turned to Sheriff Sanders and said, "As long as you and your men will back me up as I've asked, Sheriff, we should be fine."

"You can bet your life on it, Miss Hattie. We'll not fail you. I promise!" Making his way to the door, he looked back and tipped his hat. "Good day to you ladies."

Walking with Matthew out of the parlor, the Sheriff pulled Matthew aside in the grand foyer. Looking back toward the parlor, he made sure that no one could hear him, and then in a hushed voice, he said, "Matt, there's somethin' I need to talk to you about."

"Okay," Matthew responded casually, "what do you need?"

"Well, it's Ira," the Sheriff continued quietly. "He wanted me to ask you if you would come see him tonight."

"Oh, I don't know, Sheriff, I'm pretty sure Hattie won't want to leave with it being Rebecca and Lou's first night back and all."

"Alone," the Sheriff repeated, still in a whisper. "He wants to see you alone, Matt."

"I don't understand."

"Neither did I, but Ira was very emphatic about it." Looking back in the direction of the parlor, the Sheriff was getting nervous. "Look, I don't know what his reasons are. All I know is he said to make sure that Miss Hattie didn't find out."

Perplexed, Matthew didn't know what to say. He wanted to help, but he had no clue how he was going to justify a trip into town to Hattie, especially at night.

"So, what will it be?" the Sheriff asked, growing impatient.

Glancing quickly over the Sheriff's shoulder, Matthew looked at Hattie with a heavy heart. He wished so much that Ira would open up to her, but knowing that would never happen and sensing that Ira needed a friend now more than ever, Matthew sighed heavily. Turning his attention back to Sheriff Sanders, he said solemnly, "I'll be there."

Chapter 5
THE BITTER TRUTH

MAKING HIS WAY through the dark, abandoned streets of Gallatin, Matthew was nervous. He didn't know what to expect from his upcoming meeting with Ira, and though he tried to remain optimistic, he couldn't help but feel like bad news was on the horizon. As he dismounted his horse in front of the jail, the moon cast an eerie glow on the entrance, giving Matthew the chills. Making his way through the old stone doorway, his apprehension increased.

Matthew had spoken to Ira alone several times before, but tonight, as the Sheriff let him into Ira's cell, things were very different. There was a quiet desperation displayed in Ira's demeanor that Matthew had never seen before. Matthew noticed it immediately in his eyes. They moved back and forth at a frantic pace and, like the jail itself on this mid-December night, they appeared hollow and cold. With the Sheriff leaving them alone to talk, Ira shook Matthew's hand violently and invited him to sit down.

Taking a seat in the rickety, wooden chair in the corner of the tiny jail cell, Matthew watched in amazement as Ira rubbed his hands together anxiously while pacing back and forth. Sitting silent, Matthew likened him to a pot of water about to boil over. "Ira," Matthew started cautiously, "why did you have me come here tonight? Are you okay?"

"Yes and no," he replied quickly. "I mean I feel alright physically, but inside I've been going crazy lately. I keep having these horrible nightmares, and I have tell you Matt, it's almost more than I can take. I just had to talk to somebody, and with all the kindness you've shown me in the past, I figured that I could trust you." Pausing, Ira stopped and looked at Matthew with desperate eyes. "I can trust you, can't I?"

"Absolutely."

Letting out a deep sigh of relief, Ira's face showed a sudden sign of peace. Hearing Matthew's reassuring voice soothed him significantly, and as Ira took a seat on the bed across from Matthew, his extreme anxiety faded into a calmer yet very somber attitude. After a minute of silence, Ira chose his words carefully. "How's Hattie? She didn't give you any trouble about going out tonight, did she?"

"It wasn't easy explaining why I needed to come to town tonight, no, if that's what you mean. But with a little help from Mary and the fact that Hattie's preoccupied with Rebecca and Lou, I did it and I'm here. As far as Hattie goes, she's your wife, Ira. She loves you."

"My wife, yes, love me?" Ira shook his head. "Hattie loves everyone. Any feelings of true love for me disappeared long ago, I'm sure."

"I didn't say she was in love with you, Ira. I only said she loves you. She's concerned about your well-being, and she's dying for you to open up to her."

Shaking his head again, much more emphatic this time, Ira replied, "No way, Matt. I can't do that. Not now, not ever."

"Why?" Matthew asked, perplexed.

"I just can't, okay. It's very complicated. I wish there was a way it could be different, but it can't." Sitting silent for a moment, Ira thought back to the horrible events that led up to Nick's murder. He watched as the same horrifying images that had been consuming his dreams unfolded before him again and again in his mind. Realizing that if he didn't pull himself together, he would come apart, Ira quickly awakened himself from the torture of his memory. Looking about anxiously, his breathing had quickened significantly, and as he surveyed the cold, cramped quarters of the jail, he turned to Matthew with a new look of fear in his eyes. "I've always believed in God, Matt," Ira stated emphatically. "I was saved when I was a youngster and everything. But now, I feel that the sins of my past have caught up to me, and if there really is a Heaven and a Hell, it's Hell I'm bound for just as surely as I sit here."

"I don't understand why you keep saying that, Ira. It started during the trial and hasn't stopped since. If you're innocent of Nick's murder as you've said you are, what have you done that you're so concerned about?"

Ira looked away. "I may as well have killed him. Believe me, there were times I really wanted to. But it doesn't matter, I guess, because in the end Nick actually believed it was me who shot him."

"Are you saying that you were there when he was shot?"

"Yes."

Moving to the edge of his seat, Matthew could hardly believe what he was hearing. "Then you know who fired the shots that killed him?" he asked anxiously.

"Yes, Matt, I do. I wish to God I didn't, but I do."

"Why in the world haven't you said who it was?"

"I couldn't. Like I said earlier, it's more complex than you could ever imagine, and the truth, if it ever got out, could devastate the lives of so many. That is why if I tell you now, you have to promise me that you'll never tell anyone . . . ever."

"So you are protecting someone, just as we all thought?"

"Yes, I am, and if you promise me on your honor that you'll never tell anyone, I'll tell you who it is." Looking Matthew straight in the eyes, Ira asked very seriously, "Do you promise?"

"Yes."

"Good, but before I do, I want you to know that I have broken every commandment in the Bible, including 'thou shalt not kill'. So, even though I didn't kill Nick, if I am hung, believe me, I deserve it."

Listening intently, Matthew was devastated, finally realizing how Ira actually felt. "I believe, Ira," he replied compassionately, "that most sins are forgivable. After all, God is a fair and loving God. He understands the human heart, and He alone knows what your life has been."

"Do you really believe that?"

"With all my heart! Remember, I'm your friend, and whatever it is you've done, it doesn't matter to me. I would never take it upon myself to judge you."

Ira sat quietly for several moments. Matthew's sincere kindness was exactly what he needed, and though he didn't know how Matthew would react to hearing the truth about Nick's death, he felt he could trust him to keep his secret. "I appreciate your optimism, Matt, but you don't know the half of things, so I think you ought to hold off on absolving me until I finish telling you 'the bitter truth'."

Clearing his throat, Ira began slowly. "It was very cold that horrible night of November 24th. I can still remember the bite of the freezing wind on my face as I rode away from Silver Creek. As I'm sure you recall, Hattie and I had just had a horrible fight, and I left in a fury. When I look back on it now, I shouldn't have gotten angry with Hattie, she wasn't to blame that night. Heck, she was never to blame for any of our arguments. I was just frustrated to death with Nick's wanting to control every facet of my life and my not being able to break free from him. I don't know what it was, Matt, but from the moment I met him, it was almost as if he held a spell over me. I got lost in his charm, and before I knew it, I was accompanying him to some of the most extravagant and prestigious parties in all of Kansas City. He introduced me as his son, and he really treated me as if I was his own. In addition to the parties, he showered me with lavish gifts and an unending flow of money. He showed me a side of myself that I never knew existed, and even though I wasn't very worldly when we first met, he took me under his wing and turned me into a sophisticated, well-mannered man. Now, I don't expect you to understand the nature of our relationship because I don't even fully understand it to this day. All I know is that in the beginning, he made me feel good. Our being together in the way that we were helped me to forget about my insecurities and helped to give me a fresh perspective on life. But as wonderful as things started out, everything quickly turned sour, as he soon changed, and his true colors came shining through."

"What changed?"

Stopping momentarily only to wrap himself in a blanket from his bed, Ira continued as Matthew sat intrigued. "Like I said, the first six months were wonderful, as Nick took me under his wing and taught me how to act and speak correctly, and he had me believing in the fact that I could really be somebody. Shortly after that, however, Nick told me that to demonstrate my loyalty, I needed to perform 'certain duties' for him. I didn't know what he meant at first, but being young and naïve, I trusted him. You would have thought at nineteen I would have been wiser, but like I said earlier, I wasn't very worldly and Nick, to me, was larger than life. I wish to God that I would have had someone like you back then, Matt, a good friend my own age to be a sounding board for me about things, but the sad fact is, I didn't. So, with the nature of our relationship getting more complex and involved everyday, and with all the many things that he was doing for me piling up, I felt obligated to do whatever he wanted. What I didn't know at that time and have grown to regret now is that I trusted the wrong person. I thought because he was older and more experienced that he knew what he was doing. I soon found out, though, that he was only out for one person from the start . . . himself."

Thoroughly enthralled in all that Ira was telling him, Matthew leaned forward and politely interrupted. "What kind of duties did he make you do?"

"Oh, in the beginning it was nothing too serious. He would have me steal something here or lie to someone there, but then one day out of the blue, he announces that he wants me to get close to this very rich woman in Kansas City and find out all about her financial holdings. I didn't know exactly what Nick had planned, but because I trusted him, I did it. Using all that Nick had taught me, I had her charmed within days, and a couple months later, we married, allowing me access to all of her most private information."

"What happened next?" Matthew asked as he listened in amazement.

"Well," Ira replied matter-of-factly, "from there things quickly took a turn for the worst. Nick convinced me that the only way we could keep living the lifestyle that we were living was for me to skim large quantities of money from my new wife's many financial interests. It was working too, until one day when she figured out what I was doing. She went out for the day, only to return much earlier than expected, and she saw me snooping through her business files in her study. Upon entering the room, she immediately confronted me about it and got very angry when she figured out what I had been doing. I just froze until I remembered the plan Nick and I had formulated a few weeks earlier for just such an event. He had given me a vial of an unknown liquid that I was to use on her to knock her out if I felt that things were getting out of control, and not knowing what to do when she walked in on me that day, I used it."

"What happened?" Matthew asked, hardly able to contain his curiosity.

Hanging his head, Ira's voice echoed eerily through the silence. "She died."

Matthew was stunned. "Died, what do mean she died?"

"Well, as it turned out, the liquid that Nick gave me was actually a lethal yet undetectable poison. I didn't know this until after the fact, and I could have killed Nick for lying to me. But in true Starr fashion, he told me it was better that she was dead. In financial terms, he was right, because as her sole heir, I inherited everything she had, leaving Nick and I very rich."

"Unbelievable," Matthew responded, his jaw hanging ajar.

"I know, I felt just like you do, dumbfounded. Nick had purposely given me poison with the hopes that I would have to use it. I never wanted to hurt her, much less kill her, and no amount of money, nor the fact that the local Sheriff couldn't prove anything against me, held any consolation. The fact of the matter is that she died by my own hands, and there isn't a night that goes by that I don't regret her death."

"So why did you stay with Nick after all this happened? Didn't you want to get away from him?"

"God, yes, very much!"

"Why didn't you?"

"Well, the first time I threatened to leave, Nick told me he would go straight to the Kansas City Sheriff with the poison. The Sheriff had already questioned me at length about her death, and Nick said that the poison along with his testimony would be more than enough evidence to put me away. Because the Sheriff was an old friend of Nick's, he had kept everything concerning the investigation very quiet as a favor, but at the same time, I knew that if Nick wanted me charged with murder, the Sheriff would have only been too happy to oblige, whether he had the evidence or not. Then, to make matters worse, Nick told me that if I didn't give him control over all of the money I had inherited, he would still go to the Sheriff. I had no choice. I had to do what he wanted."

"I had no idea."

"No one does, Matt. You're the first person that I've ever told this to, but if you think what I've told you so far is crazy, wait till you hear the rest."

Settling back in his chair, Matthew took a deep breath. "All right, Ira, I'm listening, please continue."

"Like I was saying, with Nick threatening to turn me in, I had no choice but to do what he wanted. In the weeks following the murder, things gradually settled down, and even though I was still shook up about the whole thing, Nick convinced me with his smooth talking that things had really worked out for the best. We resumed a somewhat normal routine, and with our now limitless funds, we enjoyed a very comfortable lifestyle. Then, one day, just when I was starting to feel better about things again, Nick picked up a paper with Hattie on the front page. When I saw it, I made the mistake of commenting that I knew Hattie, which I must say, I am still regretting to this day."

Making the mental connection, Matthew said, "So that's what led you and Nick back to Gallatin, isn't it? He had already selected his next victim."

"Exactly. As soon as Nick read the extensive article on Hattie and how much money she had, he was mesmerized. He made me tell him everything about her, including my relationship with her, which, to his delight, was closer than he ever could have ever imagined. I told him all about our prospective engagement, which had happened the previous year, before I had ever met him. And at the time that I made that promise to Hattie, I really did want to marry her. Unfortunately, so much happened during my time in Kansas City that any real feelings of love toward Hattie had dissolved, as my relationship with Nick changed everything.

To me, these happenstance events were the worst thing that could have happened, but Nick, on the other hand, was thrilled. He could hardly contain himself, and he immediately began making plans to use me to get Hattie's fortune. He was already rich beyond most people's wildest dreams, but no matter how much he had, it was never enough. In the end, all he could eat, sleep, and drink was the thought of having more. Greed consumed him, and he became obsessed. He considered Hattie's immense fortune to be the pinnacle of his legacy, but in reality, it was the culmination of his downfall. He lost everything including his life over it, and now, because of my involvement, I will lose mine too."

Sitting silent, Matthew could only shake his head. Hearing the painful details concerning his life with Nick, he couldn't help but feel for Ira. Leaning out of his chair for a moment, he tried to show compassion by patting Ira on the shoulder.

Wrapping himself tighter in his blanket, Ira struggled to smile. "I appreciate your kindness, Matt, but I'm nowhere near finished. It gets even worse and more complicated." After waiting for Matthew to sit down again, Ira continued. "Now that you know all about the events in Kansas City, I think I should get back to where I started this story . . . the night of Nick's death."

"Like I said earlier, I had just had a fight with Hattie, and I went immediately to see Nick. Finally reaching my breaking point, I wanted out. I didn't care what he threatened to do to me. I wasn't going to continue to participate in anything unlawful."

"Like poisoning Hattie?" Matthew interrupted pointedly.

Seeing that Matthew knew about the poisoning, Ira hung his head in shame. "Yes, Matt, like poisoning Hattie." Without looking up, his voice was weak. "How did you know?"

"How I know is not important," Matthew replied firmly. "What I would like to know is why? Even with your own life being threatened, why put Hattie's life in danger? Did she mean that little to you?"

Seeing the intense look on Matthew's face, Ira knew this was a touchy issue to him. Choosing his words carefully, he said, "No, she didn't mean that little to me, Matt. Even though I didn't love her as I once did, I still cared a lot for her, and it was killing me to have to do what I did to her."

"Then, why?"

"It's not as simple as it looks, Matt, but you're right. I should've been stronger. I wasn't, however, and that is why I went to North Dakota. I thought if I could go somewhere where no one could ever find me that everything would somehow be okay, but unfortunately, Nick found me and threatened to kill my family if I didn't go back and help him get his hands on Hattie's fortune. So, in the end, even though I didn't care what he did to me, I still had my family to worry about."

Hearing about the threats on Ira's family, Matthew settled back down in his chair with a renewed sense of compassion for him. "I'm sorry, Ira, I shouldn't have questioned you like that. You've been through so much, and here I am giving you the third degree."

"Look, Matt," Ira replied softly, "you don't have to apologize. I'm not blind. I know how much Hattie means to you. It's been obvious to me for some time that there are deep feelings between the two of you, and in truth, I hope that someday someone like you can make Hattie happy where I couldn't. God knows she deserves that much."

Nodding his head, Matthew couldn't help but feel sheepish. He had hoped that his feelings for Hattie had gone unnoticed, but it was clear now that they had not. Deciding to change the subject, Matthew encouraged Ira to continue his story.

"Well, as I was saying, I was on my way from Silver Creek to see Nick, when I thought I was being followed. Not wanting anyone to know about my meeting with Nick, I stopped off at the small farmhouse and switched horses before making my way to see Nick at our appointed rendezvous point off the road near Bill Sharpe's farm. I was absolutely furious over what he was demanding I do to Hattie, and I had finally had enough. I didn't care what he did to me. My intentions were to tell him for once and for all that it was over."

"What about Nick's threats?"

"Yes, I thought about that very thing while I was riding through the bitter cold, and I decided right then and there that I needed a plan. Thinking quickly, I decided that if Nick wouldn't listen to reason then I was going to go to the Sheriff and tell him everything in order to protect my family. Even if I went to jail for my involvement, I figured that my family would be safe. Pausing, Ira sighed. "That, at least, was the plan."

"Things didn't go as planned, did they?"

"No, Matt, they didn't. Not by a long shot. When I approached on my horse to the spot where Nick and I were to meet, I was shocked to see not only Laville talking with Nick but also Newton and the Garlands."

"Really?" Matthew sat straight up, intrigued.

"It was a shock to me too, believe me. First of all, the meeting was supposed to be between Nick and I alone, so seeing Laville was a shock in itself. Seeing Newton, Jess, and Abner, though, was even worse and made me absolutely furious. I jumped off my horse and made my way directly over to Nick to find out what was going on. It was not like Nick to enlist the help of so many people, especially considering the high stakes, but without telling me, he had done just that."

"Why?"

"Nick's plan to take over Hattie's fortune had become such an obsession to him that he was willing to do anything to guarantee its success. Knowing how Newton, Jess, and Abner felt, he told me they were the perfect partners to complete the daunting task of getting to Hattie's fortune. I immediately objected to the whole sordid mess, telling Nick we had already made a mistake in involving Laville. Involving Newton and the Garlands was, in my opinion, the worst thing we could do."

"What did he say?"

"They all told me that if I knew what was good for me, I would be quiet. Abner even pulled a knife on me, but Nick quickly told him to put his knife away and tried to reason with me. He said that while I was absent they had all agreed that the only way to get to Hattie's fortune was to kill Hattie, James, and Lou. Nick maintained that the only way we could accomplish that was with their help."

"What happened next?" Matthew was hanging on every word.

"To my amazement, they started arguing about how they were going to disburse Hattie's fortune between themselves. Laville was very angry over her share, which was to be far less than she had anticipated, and as tempers flared, I realized that in all the craziness I had forgotten what I had come there to do in the first place, which was to tell Nick it was over."

"What did you do?"

"After listening to all I could take, I stood up and screamed at the top of my lungs, 'Enough!'. Then, turning to Nick, I said in a fury of anger that it was over and that I would have nothing more to do with any plot that would hurt anyone. I went on to tell him that I hated the way that he had controlled me for the last two years and that I never wanted to see him again."

"What did he say?"

"He didn't say anything. With his eyes aflame with rage, he got up, walked to me, drew his revolver, and pointed it directly at my head. Without blinking an eye, I told him that I didn't care what he did to me any longer. Furthermore, I told him that if he felt that shooting me was the only way for our relationship to end then so be it."

Matthew's mouth sat agape, as he listened intently to the amazing details of Ira's story. Waiting patiently, his eyes begged Ira to continue.

"So there we stood for several moments, motionless, with his gun placed squarely between my eyes. I can still remember how the cold steel of his revolver felt upon my forehead. I honestly thought it was over right then and there, and in some ways, I actually wanted him to kill me. Anything, I figured, would be better than continuing to live in the hell of fear and guilt that I was feeling."

"So what happened?" Matthew asked, unable to contain his curiosity any longer.

"To my surprise, as he readied himself to pull the trigger, we heard something move in the brush behind us. Before we could turn to look and see what it was, a gunshot rang out, striking Nick in the shoulder and knocking his gun out of his hands. I hit the ground, not knowing what was going on, only to look up and see Phillip Langley, Nick's nephew, emerge from the brush with his gun drawn. Pointing his gun in the direction of Laville, Newton, and the Garlands, he said, 'Don't move, I've got unfinished business with Nick, and I intend to see it through tonight.' Looking back at Nick, Philip said, 'Damn you Nick. It wasn't enough that you ruined my life, now you're trying to ruin other people's lives too. Well, I'm not going to allow it. Your days of causing pain are over.'"

"Ira, what happened next?"

"This is where things really got crazy. Just as Phillip raised his revolver to deliver the final blow to Nick's mortality, everyone was shocked to hear a buggy approaching. Looking to see who it was, Phillip took his eyes off Nick for a split second, giving Nick just enough time to reach into his boot and grab his spare revolver. Before Phillip even realized what Nick was doing, Nick had gotten off two shots, one striking Phillip in the leg, forcing him to limp back into the brush. As Nick slowly got to his feet, Laville ran toward him, screaming in anger, 'What are you doing? He's getting away. Go after him.' From this point, I can only guess what Nick was thinking because instead of doing what Laville told him, he turned to her and said, 'Don't push me bitch. I've had enough of you and your big mouth. You've turned out to be more problems than you're worth. If you don't shut up, I'll shoot you too.' Lifting his revolver, he pointed it at her."

"What did she do?"

"You know Laville; she went absolutely ballistic. She said, 'How dare you talk to me that way you ungrateful horse's ass. Without me, you wouldn't be half as close to getting that fortune. I have half a mind to shoot you myself.' Opening up her dress, she pulled out a revolver of her own. At this point, the buggy that was approaching had made its way to the side of the road very near to us. Realizing who was off to the side of the road, one of the occupants yelled, 'Lordy be, Lass, it be Laville, and that dog, Mr. Nick, he be goin' to shoot your sister.'"

"Wait a minute!" Matthew cried out as he nearly fell out of his chair.

"Are you telling me what I think you're telling me? Mary was there that night?"

"Yes, Matt, she was. And so was Dakota."

"That's impossible," he replied with unbelief. "I remember that night clearly, and they were in bed. How could they have been there on the side of the road if they were in bed?"

"Mary told me later in privacy that when she and Dakota heard how I had left the house that night in a rage, they immediately wanted to know what happened. Listening outside the parlor to Hattie talking with James about the details of our argument, they were shocked to hear Hattie say that she was worried about my state of mind and that she thought I might be angry enough to kill Nick. Dakota, being very intuitive, immediately felt that something bad was about to happen, and she wanted to do something. Knowing she couldn't go out into the night alone, she enlisted Mary's help to convince everyone in the mansion that they were going to bed early and then, later, to help her sneak out and drive her toward Gallatin looking for me, at which point they came upon us on the side of the road."

Pausing, Ira sighed. "I wish to God that they hadn't showed up, but the simple fact is that they did. And because they did, everything quickly went from bad to worse. Newton, Abner, and Jess, fearing they would be spotted, mounted their horses and scattered like a covey of quail. Nick, shocked to hear Mary's voice, knew that the party was over and turned to run into the brush, but Laville, still seething over their fight raised her revolver to shoot him. Fearing that in her enraged state Laville really would shoot Nick, I jumped to my feet, ran toward her, and dove at her just as she pulled the trigger. She managed to get an errant shot off before I wrestled the gun from her, at which point she took off running into the brush. Getting to my feet, I started after her only to stop when I heard two more gun shots from behind. Looking up, I saw Nick fall into a heap on the ground, and when I turned around to see where the shots came from, I got the greatest shock of my life, as there, standing up in her buggy with rifle still drawn, was Dakota Jayne. Through her keen sense of hearing, she had obviously placed everyone in her mind, and after she heard the first shot ring out, she took aim in the direction of Nick's footsteps and shot him. Mary was beside herself, as she yelled, 'Oh, Lass, you've killed Mr. Nick in cold blood; they'll hang you for sure!' Dakota then fainted and Mary sped their buggy back to Silver Creek, but the damage was done."

Thoroughly amazed, Matthew asked, "What did you do after that?"

"Well, first I looked for Laville, and not seeing her, I decided the most important thing was to get Dakota back to Silver Creek, so without a second thought, I mounted my horse and caught up to Mary in the buggy. I rode with her to the front drive of the estate, where I knew she would be safe, and I told her to get Dakota back into the house as quickly as possible. Then, still not knowing if Nick was dead or alive, I went back to the side of the road to see if he was still there. When he wasn't, I figured that he must not have been shot as badly as I had thought, and I decided it would be best to get as far away from there as possible, lest anyone saw me near the road where all those gunshots went off. From that point, still being pretty shook up about everything, I rode my horse aimlessly for several hours, trying to make sense of all that had happened. Finally, at a little after three in the morning, I went home, slipped into bed, and lay awake, dreading the morning."

Totally in awe of everything he just heard, Matthew didn't know what to say. Getting to his feet, he walked to the window, and after gazing out at the stars for a minute, he spoke somberly, "As crazy as this story is, Ira, I really do believe you. I must admit, though, that there are still a lot of things that don't make sense to me. For instance, why hasn't Dakota said anything in all this time about your innocence?"

"She doesn't remember, Matt. She suffered some sort of amnesia that night and doesn't remember a thing. Mary took her to see Doc Cowley about her memory loss, and without telling him exactly what happened, she got a diagnosis. He said that she was definitely suffering from clinical amnesia, and though in most cases the memory comes back in days, there are cases of amnesia surrounding a traumatic incident where the person's memory never returns. Thankfully, I feel that we're dealing with the latter because she hasn't remembered yet. I know there are people that would think me crazy for hanging for a crime I didn't commit, but I've gone to great lengths to protect Dakota throughout this whole horrible affair. And I'm not going to stop until I see it through. She was an innocent bystander who got caught up in a bad situation, and she doesn't deserve to get in trouble for something that I could've prevented."

Matthew was stunned. Hearing Ira finish his story, everything was finally making sense. He knew now what Ira had meant when he said that the truth could ruin the lives of so many. Making his way to Ira's bedside he tried in some small way to offer consolation. Reaching out his hand, his voice was tender. "I'm sorry. I had no idea."

Hanging his head for a moment, Ira tried to not let his emotions get the best of him. Summoning his voice, he said, "Don't feel too badly for me, Matt. I deserve to walk the path I'm on. Just knowing about the way I was poisoning Hattie should convince you of that. I've committed many horrors, and no matter what I do or say, there is no denying that many people have been severely hurt by my actions. That is why I told you to hold off on absolving me until you knew the whole truth. I never wanted to hurt Hattie, that's the truth, but I know now that by doing nothing to stop Nick, I was just as guilty as he was. It's kind of like my father used to say, 'Making no choice is still making a choice.' And the repercussions of that choice are more than I can bear. Oh, now how I wish I had listened to my father's good advice"

"Now, Ira, don't be so hard on yourself," Matthew replied sympathetically. "Nick had you trapped. You reacted the best you knew how to under the circumstances."

"Did I, though?" Ira replied quickly. Everyday for the last year I've asked myself that question, and the answer I always come up with is that I didn't do my best under the circumstances. I didn't even come close. There are a million things I could have and should have done different, but I didn't. I failed miserably, and now I'm getting exactly what I deserve."Feeling deep compassion for Ira, Matthew stood silent. It seemed as though there was nothing that he could say to make Ira feel better about the way that things turned out, but yet in spite of everything, Matthew felt he needed to continue to offer his support. Taking a seat next to him on the bed, he embraced him as a brother would. "We don't always know exactly why things happen the way they do, Ira," Matthew said kindly. "Only God knows that." Separating himself slightly, he looked into Ira's tear-blurred eyes. "We are put here on the earth by Him to be tested, and even though it may seem like you have failed miserably, growth is measured in many different ways. For example, through this whole sordid mess, can you honestly tell me that you aren't a better person now than you were before you met Nick?"

"No."

"You see what I mean. Even though the things you have gone through have been horrible, I bet that you've learned a lot, haven't you?"

"Well, yes, I guess I have."

"You're darn right you have! First and foremost, you've learned not to trust every person who comes around the pike because more times than not they're only out for themselves. Secondly, you've learned that even though you have money and power, it can't buy you happiness or peace, and most of all, you learned that running from a problem will never make it go away. In fact, running only makes your problems worse. If you ask me, you've been blessed in a number of ways because you know now what type of person you don't want to be."

"Really?"

"Absolutely, my father has always been very adamant to me about death being nothing more than a right of passage into another, greater reality. It is not an ending like most people think. Instead, he likened death to being the ultimate beginning rather than a horrible ending, and you, Ira, because of your trials in this life will go into that new reality with a much better perspective than someone who hasn't experienced as much as you have. It's all in how you look at things, really." Pausing, Matthew took a deep breath. "I know you don't feel very good about the way things turned out now, but people make mistakes everyday. And a lot worse than the ones you've told me about. The wonderful thing about God is that no matter how badly you screw up, as long as pray to Him with a contrite spirit and a broken heart, He will forgive you. And I have no doubt that if you do that, you will be accepted into Heaven."

***

LATER THAT NIGHT, after Matthew had gone home, Ira lay on his bed, thinking of the things he had told him. Closing his eyes, he felt like a great weight had been lifted from his shoulders. Their friendship, Ira thought, as he stared at the ceiling of his tiny jail cell, was the best thing that had ever happened to him. "Funny," he thought, "that a friendship as rare as Matt's can become a part of life's bittersweet refrain."

Chapter 6
THE LAST GOODBYE

FOR THE FIRST TIME in her life, Hattie actually dreaded the dawn of every new morning. With Ira's hanging scheduled for the 28th of December, a dark cloud hung over the holiday season. Having Rebecca and Lou back at Silver Creek helped her to pass the time and stay occupied in a somewhat normal routine, but with every passing day, Hattie knew she was one day closer to the inevitable.

Right up to the last, Ira and Mary remained in a constant state of worry. They feared that Dakota would suffer a mental breakdown if her memory returned. Unlike Hattie, Ira awaited each morning with great anticipation, as it meant that he was one day closer to putting an end to the craziness that had consumed his life for so long. Ira knew that once he was hung for the murder, no one else could be convicted, and Mary promised she would work through the trauma with Dakota, if her memory ever did return.

Christmas Eve and morning came and went, bringing with them little solace. Everyone was congenial and at times even lighthearted, but more times than Hattie wanted to count, the conversation returned to Ira and his impending doom.

On the night of December 27, with time quickly closing in on her, Hattie decided to see Laville in one final attempt to get the truth, but before she could leave, Minerva met at the back entry near the kitchen.

"Hattie, Honey, surely you're not headed for Laville's at this time of the night?"

"Yes, Mama, I am!"

"Oh please, Dear, not tonight. You're too worn out. You'll just end up in a quarrel." Taking her daughter's hand, Minerva was very concerned. "I worry about you meeting with Laville, Hattie. I'm always afraid she'll make you so mad, you'll wind up killing her. God knows I wouldn't blame you, but I worry nonetheless."

"Oh, for heaven's sake, Mama, I won't get that mad." Stroking her mother's cheek, she spoke reassuringly. "I promise." Turning, Hattie walked to the hall closet, reached in, and took out her 45's. Putting them carefully in the holsters inside her dress, she turned again to see her mother's disappointment. "Now Mama, stop worrying. Don't you understand? I've got to talk to Laville, and I must do it tonight. Ira's hanging is tomorrow, and I must know the truth."

Arriving in town and driving up in front of Laville's lavish home, which now belonged to her, Hattie took a deep breath. Matthew, who, along with Shannon, had accompanied her to town on this cold, blustery night, helped her out of the carriage and walked with her as she carefully made her way up the snow-covered walk.

Knocking on the door, she saw the figure of little Sarah Showalter coming down the hall.

The door opened, and Sarah gave Hattie a big smile. "Good evenin', Miss Hattie, is Miss Laville expectin' you?"

"No, Sarah, she isn't. Would you be good enough to tell her I'm here?"

Sarah turned, walked to the bottom of the stairs, and was starting to go up them just as Laville appeared on the landing. Hattie had no more than stepped inside the house and was just taking off her cape when she heard Laville's voice.

"Needn't take that cape off, Hattie. You won't be staying long enough in my home to get warm, I assure you!"

"As I recall, Laville," Hattie quipped right back, "this house and everything in it, belongs to me now."

"Oh . . . well, I suppose it is, but I don't remember asking to see you, so why in the hell are you here?"

Hattie had always hated that indignant tone in Laville's voice. Looking up the stairs, she watched Laville descending in an exquisite dress of the latest fashion, with her hair piled high up on her head. "How," Hattie wondered, "can she be so beautiful and so damn evil at the same time?"

Pausing midway down stairs, Laville said, "I'm asking again, Hattie, just why in the hell are you here?"

Looking at Laville in disgust, Hattie didn't give a response. Instead she motioned for Matthew and Shannon to wait outside.

Dismissing Sarah as she reached the bottom of the stairs, Laville said, "Your Pa will be arriving any minute, Sarah. Go outside and wait for him." Then, grabbing her tiny arm just as she was walking away, Laville added, "And be sure you're here by seven tomorrow morning to help me dress. I want to look my best for the hanging."

"Want me to tell Pa hello for you, Miss Laville?"

"Tell him any damn thing you please! I could care less."

"There's no need to be rude to the child, Laville."

"Don't you dare march in here and tell me what to say, Hattie!"

Putting on her ragged little coat, Sarah excused herself to Miss Hattie, and left as quickly as she could, closing the front door behind her.

Biting her tongue to control her anger, Hattie took a deep breath. She hated the way Laville acted, but wanting to talk to Laville about

Nick's death, she knew she would have to look past her deplorable behavior. "Could we go in the parlor and talk, Laville?"

"About what?"

"About Ira."

"That," Laville snipped, "is a dead subject!"

Hattie let the remark go and continued to try to be as civil as she could. "Please, Laville, calm down. I assure you that I'm here under the best of intentions."

"You listen to me, Hattie. I'm not interested in the least as to what your intentions are. I have absolutely no use for that damned Ira and very little for you."

Try as Hattie did to remain composed, Laville's attitude really angered her. "Don't talk to me like that, Laville! Not after all I've done for you. You seem to have forgotten that I've spent a fortune on you and handed you enough money to buy this whole damn town. I think that at the very least you could be civil when I want to talk to you."

"Oh, all right, talk if you must. But before you do, I want you to know that as far as I'm concerned, whatever you've done for me is very little in comparison to the millions you have! One would think you'd want to help people with all that money. You know, do something out of the goodness of your heart."

"You're a fine one to talk, Laville. I doubt very seriously if there's one ounce of goodness in your heart. As a matter of fact, I wonder if you have a heart at all. And if you do, I'll bet it's as black as the darkest night."

"Well, pure heart, black heart, or no heart at all, what the hell does it matter to you?"

"Please, Laville, for just one night in our lives, let's stop sparing. What have I ever done to you to bring out this hostility toward me?"

Ignoring her question, Laville's patience was wearing thin. "Hattie, get to the point. I don't have all night. What the hell are you here for?"

Speaking firmly, Hattie wanted answers. "I want to know the truth about Nick's murder, Laville. I've heard all your lies, and I'm sick of them. I'm not letting Ira go to his grave without my knowing the truth. So I'm asking you for the last time, do you know who killed Nick?"

"Yes, I do," Laville replied indignantly, "and so does Ira."

Drawing out her revolvers, Hattie pointed them at Laville. "When I left the house tonight, I promised Mama I wouldn't kill you, Laville, but I didn't promise her that I wouldn't ruin your looks or make you a cripple."

Using her usual theatrics, Laville stepped back and clutched her heart with one hand and placed the other over her brow. "Do you mean to tell me that you actually discussed shooting me with my own mother?"

"Our mother, Laville, *our* mother! And I'll have you know she said she dreaded the thought that I might kill you, but said she wouldn't blame me if I did. Now, do you have the faintest idea of the pain I've suffered?"

Laville couldn't believe what she just heard. "Oh, please, Hattie, don't start! If I've heard it once, I've heard it a thousand times. Poor little Hattie, born talented, beautiful, and now rich beyond her wildest dreams, and she's still upset because she can't get everything she wants."

"Shut up, Laville! You're beginning to sound and act just like Pa. You waltz through life wreaking havoc, spreading pain, and not giving a damn who you hurt."

"All right!" Laville screamed. "You think you're so damn smart. Yet, you can't see the truth even when it's right under your pretty little nose. Pa, Jess, and Abner are just a few people who had it in for Nick.

I'd suggest if you really want to know the truth, get Mary Walsh off alone and talk to her. She knows the truth, but I'll guarantee you that it'd be easier getting blood from a stone than the truth out of her. Now if you don't like those answers, just shoot me."

"Don't tempt me, Laville. Nothing would make me happier than to put a bullet right through those pearly white teeth of yours." Laville grew faint as Hattie pushed her backward into the parlor and down onto the settee in the middle of the room. "What do you mean, 'ask Mary'? What in the world would Mary Walsh know about Nick's murder?"

"She knows everything!" Laville snarled.

Shaking her head emphatically, Hattie refused to believe what Laville was saying. "Stop your lying, Laville. Mary is a good person. How can you sit there and drag her into this? If anyone in our family looks guilty, it's you. You stood to gain the most from Nick's death."

"Oh, really," Laville smirked. "Well, you can't prove a thing, so you can kiss that idea goodbye."

"Look, Laville, all I want to know is who killed Nick? If you're as innocent as you say you are, and if you were there that night, then why on earth can't you tell me."

"Listen, Hattie, Nick Starr had more enemies than you can shake a stick at. He did a lot of people dirty before he came to Gallatin, and some of them probably followed him here."

"Then, you're saying almost anyone could have killed him?"

"Didn't you ever think of that? It's true that I stood to gain every-thing from his death, but I didn't want just his money, I wanted the pres-tige and power that went with it. I had set my sights on someday living in the White House. Like everyone else, I was positive Nick would someday be Governor of Missouri, then go to Washington as a Senator, and eventually become President. I sure as hell won't have what I wanted now that he's dead."

"Your desire all along was to be the First Lady?"

"Absolutely! Imagine what I could have done with the power of the White House behind me?"

Hattie cringed. The thought of Laville in the White House was enough to scare even the heartiest of persons. "Good heavens, Laville." Hattie replied with amazement, "is power all you ever think about?"

"Of course! And if you think for one minute I wanted Nick out of the way for his money, you're dead wrong. His money was just the tip of the iceberg."

"So if anyone could have killed Nick, how do I know you didn't have him killed?"

Laville smacked her forehead with her hand. "Go ask Mary Walsh for the truth. She and Ira know plenty about that night that they haven't told you."

"Why would Ira hold back information, Laville? It doesn't make any sense. Besides, he's a better man than that."

"Don't kid yourself, Little Sister. Your precious Ira is not the angel you would like him to be. I know enough about him to curl that pretty red hair of yours. Remember it was me who went with him first. A better man than that, ha! Believe me, you don't know Ira Saxon."

"And I suppose you do?"

"You bet your sweet buttercups I do." This was the chance Laville had been waiting for. She now had an opportunity to really hurt Hattie, and she could hardly wait. "I've been with him so many times that I can tell you everything about him, including every blemish on his body. Like the scar on his stomach below his belt or the birthmark just inside his right thigh or the mole just inches below his navel."

Hattie had heard enough. It was obvious that Laville had seen him naked. "All right, Laville, that's enough!" Hattie was sick. Ira had lied about so many things. Even now, on the eve of his death, she was still dealing with his lies. "What would compel Ira to surround himself with lies," her mind raced, "and when will they ever end?" Trying desperately to understand Laville, Hattie asked, "Why, if you once loved Ira, would you want to hurt him?"

"Love Him? Who in the Hell ever said I loved him? I said I had been with him. For hell's sake, Hattie, you're as silly as Mama. Grow up! You don't have to love a man to sleep with him."

"And why did you feel you had to tell me about you and Ira?"

"Because I hate Ira for what he did when I was married to John Anderson. Ira was the one who ruined my marriage. He tried to seduce me at a church picnic, and John saw it. Ira was such a coward and so afraid of John, he blamed the whole incident on me. That's when John left me."

Hattie couldn't believe what she was hearing. "That's ridiculous! John and Ira were good friends. I won't stand here and listen to any more of your lies."

"It doesn't matter anymore. Tomorrow Ira hangs, and there's nothing anyone can do about it. I told him I'd see he got what's coming to him, and tomorrow I will. Ha! Ha! Ha!" Getting to her feet, Laville laughed in Hattie's face. "For once in your life, Hattie Morran, you're in a mess that you can't sing, shoot, or buy your way out of. Maybe you ought to get down on your knees and try praying to God," she quipped. "Maybe He'll listen to you. But as for me, I'm sick to death of your whining. Now get out!"

Hattie stood motionless. Her heart was pounding so hard, she could hear it in her ears. Again pointing her revolvers at Laville, she cringed as Laville's maniacal laugh echoed through her mind. She struggled with herself to keep from shooting Laville, but deep down she wanted to send her straight to hell, where she belonged. Closing her eyes tightly, Hattie went over the events of the past year. Scenes from the trial flashed in her head, and after several moments, she came to realize the cold reality of the situation. As much as she hated it, Laville was right. There was no way she could stop Ira's hanging in the morning. Opening her eyes again, Hattie took a deep breath and backed up several feet.

Seeing Hattie's expressionless face, Laville stopped laughing and sheer terror set in. "Is she actually going to shoot me?" she wondered. "Don't shoot me!" she yelled in terror, as Hattie continued backing down the hall toward the front door. Looking through the parlor window, Laville could see two men coming up the front walk. Frantically, she cried out, "Help! Please help me!" The door opened, and in the doorway stood Shannon and Matthew.

"What's going on, Hattie?" Matthew asked.

"Laville told me tonight that there were many people who could have killed Nick. Evidently, he had been involved in a great number of shady deals. Laville could have mentioned this fact during the trial but didn't, of course. That fact itself could have led to a reasonable doubt and could have kept Ira from being convicted."

Looking up at Matthew and Shannon, Laville pleaded, "Don't listen to her. She's a crazy woman. Please take those damn guns away from her."

Shannon looked at his sister Hattie, then straight into Laville's cold, unfeeling eyes. "If what you say is true, Hattie, I don't care if she is our sister. Go ahead and blow her silly damn head off." Turning around, he walked out the door, and Hattie fired both guns instantaneously. In the next moment, Laville slumped to the floor. Matthew couldn't believe it. "Hattie, have you lost your mind? I thought you said you wouldn't shoot her?"

"Oh, come on, Matthew, I didn't shoot her. I just fired on either side of her, but I'll bet before she fainted, she thought she was a dead woman."

Matthew wiped the perspiration from his forehead. "I thought for sure that under all the stress, an artery must have broken loose in your brain."

"Nope, I just wanted to put the fear of God in her."

"Hattie, you've got to stop talking like that. Often if we're not careful, our thoughts become our actions." The rest of Hattie's bodyguards, hearing the gun shots, came running toward the house.

Stopping them at the porch, Shannon sent them back to their horses. "Everything's okay, Fellas, Hattie's just a little trigger-happy."

"Look, Matthew," Hattie said firmly, "I want Laville to get it through her thick head that I've had enough. I'm not going to put up with her lies and theatrics anymore."

"I'm shocked she was willing to tell you anything," Shannon said as he returned to the doorway.

"Well, it wasn't much, and unfortunately, it was far too little to save Ira. Think of it like this, if the Pearly Gates are closed as tight as Laville's mouth, none of us has a ghost of a chance of getting into Heaven." Returning her guns to their holsters in her dress, and then turning to a nearby mirror, Hattie put on her cape and lifted the hood gently over her hair. In the mirror, she could see Laville's reflection as she began to regain consciousness. "Come on, Boys, let's get out of here before she comes to and starts flapping that big mouth of hers again." Walking to her carriage and taking a seat inside, Hattie said, "Now, take me to the jail. I still want answers, and if I can't get them from Laville, then I'm going to get them from Ira."

With her face full of determination, Matthew and Shannon followed Hattie down the snow-covered walk and back to the carriage. Matthew took the reins and, surrounded by Hattie's men, they made their way quickly across town to the jail. Upon arriving, they found the Sheriff standing outside the front door. "Evenin', Miss Hattie, kind of late to be out, isn't it?" he said with a smile.

"Good Evening to you to, Sheriff," she replied as she got out her carriage. "Yes, I know it's late, but I desperately need to talk with Ira."

"Oh, I'm afraid he's not much in the talkin' mood, Miss Hattie. Like the rest of us, he's pretty discouraged about tomorrow. I was just leavin' to go check on some gunshots Ira and I heard a few minutes ago."

"Needn't bother, Sheriff," Shannon said, as he escorted his sister toward the jail. "It was Hattie, trying to scare the living hell out of Laville."

"Did you do it, Miss Hattie?"

"I doubt it. One thing I've learned about evil is that it never gives up, and Laville, I'm sorry to say, is as close to pure evil as you can get."

Inside his cell, Ira sat silent, listening to their conversation. Fearfully, he wondered what she might have found out. As Hattie entered the jail and the Sheriff let her into his cell, his voice held a very serious tone. "What did she tell you?"

"According to Laville, it seems there are a lot of people who were out to get Nick. You must have known that, Ira," she said, as the Sheriff let her into Ira's cell.

"I know how she lies," he responded quickly.

"I don't think Laville was lying this time. It's obvious to me now that there is much more that happened that night than what was previously suspected, and I've got to find out what." Getting up and standing before Hattie, Ira was furious. "You've got to leave things alone, Hattie!"

"Leave things alone and give up? Never! Not if it takes me the rest of my life! You've put me through hell, Ira Saxon, and I deserve to know the truth."

Hearing Hattie's unwavering conviction, Ira stepped back. He knew going toe to toe with Hattie was useless, but he also knew that if she kept digging, she would surely find the truth. Lowering his voice, he pleaded with her. "For God's sake, Hattie, when I'm gone, forget about it. Look for some happiness, find someone to spend the rest of your life with, and forget all of this."

"And just who would you suggest I look for to take your place?"

After taking a moment to think, he dropped his voice all the way down to a whisper. "Well, since you won't consider Matt, then why not my cousin, Walker."

Stepping back, Hattie didn't know what to say. "Walker Donovan?"

"Yes, Walker Donovan"

"Why on earth would you suggest someone like Walker Donovan?"

"Oh, come on, Hattie, don't be so stubborn. You told me yourself not too long ago that you'd thought he'd changed a lot since his youth. Besides, most importantly, like Matt, Walker cares about you."

Shaking her head emphatically, Hattie spoke firmly. "I think you are reading too much into things. Walker and I are just friends. And not even good ones at that. I hardly think that he would be someone that I would want to spend the rest of my life with."

Ira was about to respond when the Sheriff, knowing the hour was late and seeing they were quarreling, came to the cell and interjected, "Tomorrow is goin' to come pretty early for all of us, Miss Hattie, and Ira still hasn't had any supper. Maybe it would be best if you said goodnight."

Nodding in agreement, Hattie sighed. "Ira, why tonight, of all nights, are we still quarreling?" she asked, frustrated.

Ira forced a smile and stepped toward Hattie and gently pulled the hood of her cape over her hair. She was so beautiful, more beautiful than she had ever been. Looking into her eyes, he said softly, "Please remember that I will always care about you."

"I will."

"And promise me just one thing."

"What?" she asked, as she reached up, brushing a lock of his hair back from his face.

"Live a rich full life. Take that damn money of Rebecca's and do all the good you can, whenever you can, in any way you can, for as long as you can."

"I will, I promise."

"One more thing."

"Let's not push it, Ira," she said with a smile.

"Raise a family, a big family."

Laying her head against his massive chest, they held each other for one final moment in their final embrace. Looking up at him through tear-filled eyes, Hattie's voice was weak. "Oh, Ira, why couldn't things have been different?"

"Shhhh," he answered, putting his finger on her lips. "Don't dwell on it anymore. Just know that one morning, you'll wake up and find that life is all fresh and new again. And you'll meet someone, someone who will really love you." Taking her face in his, he gently kissed her forehead, then slowly stepped back and smiled.

Turning to leave, Hattie took one final look back at Ira standing in the moonlight pouring through the window in his cell. She had dreaded this moment from the day that the judge had first sentenced Ira to hang, and now as she stood motionless in the doorway, she knew that with this, 'the last goodbye', the end was at hand.

***

LATE THAT NIGHT, Laville sat anxiously looking out her parlor window. Her visit with Hattie had upset her greatly, and as she gazed out into the snow-covered streets, Laville tried to calm herself from the evening's earlier events. Finally seeing what she was looking for, Laville smiled slightly as a lone rider on horseback approached her house in the moonlight. Making her way to the door, she waited till the rider knocked then quickly opened the door and pulled him inside.

Leading the rider to the parlor, Laville invited him to sit down. Then, taking a seat opposite him, they sat for a moment in silence. Finally, seeing Laville's discouragement, the rider asked, "What in the hell happened to you? You did want to see me tonight, didn't you?"

Looking at him with very serious eyes, Laville replied, "Yes, I'm glad you showed up as planned. I've just had a bad day, that's all."

"What happened?"

"Hattie happened, Abner. She came over tonight, waving those damn pistols of hers around like a crazy woman, threatening to shoot me if I didn't tell her the truth about Nick's murder."

"So what did you tell her?"

"Well, I had to tell her something, so I told her if she wanted the truth that bad that she should ask Mary Walsh what happened that night."

"Are you crazy?" Abner responded angrily. "That damn old woman knows exactly what happened, and she could, if she wanted to, implicate both of us for being there that night."

"Oh, don't get your dander up, Abner," Laville replied quickly. "Like I told Hattie, it would be easier getting blood from a stone than getting the truth out of Mary Walsh. I'm not worried about that."

"Then what are you worried about?"

Glaring at Abner, Laville replied, "I just want to make sure everything goes as planned tomorrow. If Hattie's visit tonight proved anything to me, it's that we can't take any chances. I didn't give Stanley
Johnson all that money for nothing, and tomorrow I intend to see Ira
Saxon hang as planned, no matter what. Do you understand me, no
matter what! And you tell Stanley that if everything doesn't go as
planned, I'll have his head."

Nodding, Abner could see Laville meant business. "I'll tell him,"
he replied, "but I still don't understand your crazy vendetta against Ira.
What in the hell did he ever do to you?"

"What did he ever do to me?" Laville repeated, her eyes aflame with
anger. "I'll tell you what he did. First, he chose Hattie over me; then,
he ruined my marriage to John Anderson; and lastly and worst of all,
he wouldn't cooperate with Nick to get Hattie's fortune, causing that fi-
asco by the road, allowing Nick to get shot and die. In short, he has
single-handedly ruined all of my dreams."

"Well," Abner said matter-of-factly, "there's no reason why we can't
get our hands on Hattie's fortune ourselves."

Sitting back in her chair, Laville's rage calmed, as she slowly ran
Abner's proposal over and over in her mind. It was obvious to Abner
that she was intrigued, yet she stayed silent for quite some time before
replying cautiously. "As much as I enjoy the thought of having all that
money, Abner, I feel our chance passed us by when Nick died. Besides,
with Ira getting what he deserves tomorrow and Nick's fortune at my
disposal, I no longer have the same need nor desire to go up against
Hattie and those damn bodyguards of her. If you ask me, trying to
fight them now would not only be foolish but downright stupid."

Greatly angered by Laville's lack of support, Abner's demeanor
turned deathly cold. Looking her straight in the eyes, his voice held

deep disdain. "Well, isn't it nice that everything's worked out for you? Unfortunately, I don't have that luxury. Unlike you, I have no money, and I have not yet gotten my revenge. I still have a promise to fulfill. I told Hattie that I would make her pay for what she did to me, and I intend to fulfill that promise."

"And just what do you think you're going to do?" Laville questioned indignantly.

Smiling a sadistic smile, Abner rubbed his hands together devilishly. "Trust me. She won't even know what hit her."

Chapter 7
BITTER HARVEST

HATTIE LEFT THE JAIL that night dejected and bewildered. "How could things have come to this?" she wondered. It didn't seem fair to her that the truth about Nick's death was so successfully eluding her, and it was the constant wonder of things unknown that would haunt Hattie for years to come.

Ira, though mentally exhausted after his visit with Hattie, asked for fried eggs, squirrel, and dried peaches for supper. Mrs. Sanders was more than happy to cook his final meal for him, as she and the Sheriff had both become quite fond of Ira during his lengthy incarceration. She became quite worried, however, after serving him, as he couldn't eat more than a few bites. Realizing that Ira had a lot weighing on his mind, she sent a deputy to get Reverend Walker, and within minutes, he arrived, willing to help in any way that he could.

Ira was extremely grateful to have someone to talk to, and after about an hour of constructive conversation, Reverend Walker said goodnight for the evening. Upon leaving the jail, the Reverend pulled Sheriff Sanders outside and said, "It's amazing, Bob, I've never seen any man more resigned to his death than Ira. Whatever it was that Matthew Forsythe said to him, during his visit that you told me about, has done more good for him than anything I could have said or done. I've really been worried about the lad, but tonight he is oddly at peace about his impending death. Could a murderer be so at peace with himself, knowing that tomorrow morning his soul will be hurled into eternity?"

Shaking his head, the Sheriff leaned against the door frame. "I've spent all these months with Ira, Reverend, and never once have I believed he was guilty of killing Nick Starr. I feel so strongly about the whole thing that I would wager my life on it. That being said, I feel horrible for the Morran family, the past few years of their lives certainly have been a 'bitter harvest'."

Bidding the Reverend farewell, Sheriff Sanders returned to his desk only to hear a knock at the door. Answering it, the Sheriff was surprised to see the Forsythe brothers standing on the snowy stoop of the jail.

"Matt, Cameron, Archer, what are you doing here?"

"With your permission, we'd like to stay with Ira the rest of the night, Sheriff. As you know, my brothers and I feel that Ira is pretty much like family."

"Does Hattie know you boys are doing this?" the Sheriff asked bluntly.

"Absolutely," Matthew replied without hesitation. "We made sure she got back to Silver Creek safely, and then we asked if we could be relieved of our duties for this one night so that Ira wouldn't have to be alone. She was all for it."

The Sheriff turned to Ira, who stood dumbfounded in his cell. No one had offered to spend his last night with him, until now. Summoning his voice, he motioned to the Sheriff to let them in. "I'd be grateful, Sheriff. I really don't want to be alone."

Sheriff Sanders agreed, knowing that their presence could only help Ira, and if anyone could bring him even one ounce of comfort in this, his eleventh hour, the Sheriff was all for it.

As the Sheriff let them into Ira's cell, Ira asked quietly, "Would you men pray with me?"

"We surely will," Matthew replied emphatically. "We're here to do anything we can for you, Ira."

Following Matthew's lead, Ira knelt, followed by Cameron, Archer, and even the Sheriff. A moment later, Matthew began to pray, and throughout the night Ira was greatly comforted by his prayer, as well as the scripture reading and stories of inspiration that the Forsythe's shared with him.

Back at Silver Creek, the entire family congregated in the parlor and tried to provide solace to Ira's family. Hattie and Minerva tried to keep the conversation light and upbeat, but it was no use. Everyone knew what would be happening once morning arrived, and as such, no one got much sleep during the night. Many times there were tears, brought on by the strong feelings that the spirits of the Saxons' parents, Andrew and Samantha, had not left their family alone in this, their hour of need.

Early the next morning, the enclosure around the gallows began to fill with people, and just before eleven o' clock, Sheriff Sanders and a deputy went into Ira's cell. By law, they were forced to read the fatal document from the Circuit Court, to which Ira made no response. Then the death warrant was read. Ira went to the bars of the window, looked toward heaven and responded, "Surely this is your will, Oh Lord, so let it be done."

Sheriff Sanders, walking over and touching Ira's shoulder, said in a quivering voice, "Are you ready, Son?"

Ira picked up the book he had written about his life, along with some poems and songs, placed them in a leather bag and handed it to Matthew. "Please see that Hattie gets these." Then nodding that he was ready to go, he left his cell for the front door of the jail.

As they stepped outside, the brightness of the sun nearly blinded them. Even though it was crisp and cold outside, even with having been a light snowfall in the night, the day was surprisingly pleasant. Ira's look was without expression, as he looked into an endless sea of faces. Many held scowls, others were tear-stained, but all were there to see him serve the sentence the court had given him.

Slowly, he was escorted through the ever-increasingly hostile crowd to the gallows in the town square, with Reverend Walker following close behind.

As they reached the top of the gallows, Ira looked out over the enormous fenced enclosure, which men had been working on for days. It appeared as though there were well over seven hundred people. Beyond the high board fence, he could see concourses of people standing on what were probably a multitude of wagons, driven up behind the wall. Slowly he scanned the buildings surrounding the town square, and on the roof tops and behind windows, ghastly pale faces appeared as though they were carved in stone. "How empty they must all feel, awaiting the scene of horror, which is soon to come," he thought in amazement. The crowd quieted as Reverend Walker began reciting the Lord's Prayer from the Bible.

Sheriff Sanders, standing next to Ira, asked, "Is there anything you wish to say, Ira?"

Scanning the crowd slowly, Ira saw Hattie several rows back from the front. She was standing between Minerva and Matthew, with his arm wrapped around her. The rest of her bodyguards surrounded her on all sides. Rebecca, Lou, Lorna and the rest of the family stood silently behind them. Hattie surprised not only Ira but everyone who saw her, as she wasn't dressed in black, as one would suppose, but in an exquisite pale blue velvet dress, with a matching cape trimmed in white fur. He shook his head, thinking, "Being dressed like that is making a mighty bold statement, Hattie. Tongues will be wagging over that." At that same moment, Ira recognized several reporters scattered throughout the crowd. "They'll never let Hattie live this down," he continued thinking. From there his eyes fell on a man, who raised his fist and cursed him, and his thoughts returned to the heinous death that awaited him. And yet, it couldn't compare to the pain that he could see in his family's faces. From his sisters to his cousins, the Donovan's, everyone was having trouble controlling their emotions. As he looked past the crowd to them, he prayed silently, "Dear God, please give them the strength to get through this."

Sheriff Sanders asked Ira again if there was anything he had to say. Turning, Ira thanked him one last time for the kindness that he had shown him the past year, and then, standing up straight, he said to the crowd in a loud voice, "Ladies and Gentlemen, I tell you it is an awful thing to be hung like a dog in the street and be forced to leave my wife, family, and many of you who are my friends, but eternity and the loving arms of my parents await me."

Next, to everyone's amazement, Ira began to sing. Complete silence fell over the crowd as Ira's deep baritone voice reverberated around the makeshift enclosure. Hattie, Ira, and the family had been planning this for some time, but everyone else was left dumbfounded. Singing the words to 'Nearer My God to Thee', Ira continued until he finished the first stanza, when abruptly the crowd heard Hattie's voice joining his. Singing in perfect harmony with Ira, she slowly made her way toward the gallows, with Matthew and Cameron on either side. Before they finished the second verse, she was making her way up the steps to stand next to Ira. On the chorus, Matthew and Cameron added their voices, and from the crowd, the rest of the Morran family and Ira's sisters could be heard as well. Their voices that cold, winter day sounded like a Heavenly Choir, and here and there, as Hattie had planned, her friends sang with them. Knowing she must soften the hearts of the crowd, they repeated the chorus, and this time she called on the crowd to join them. It was sure a sight to see, as hundreds of people, mesmerized by it all, began to sing. As Hattie had hoped, tears flowed and hearts were softened as hundreds of voices reached the heavens in this, the final moments of Ira Saxon's life.

Matthew, Mary, and Laville knew that Ira was innocent, and they alone knew that he was making the ultimate sacrifice, in sacrificing his life that the life of a friend might be spared. As the song ended, Ira's gaze fell on Dakota, standing next to James. "Will she ever remember?" he wondered in vain.

With their singing over, Sheriff Sanders allowed Hattie the privilege of kissing Ira, and once again, the crowd fell deathly silent. Taking her arm, Matthew led her back down the steps to the front. Because Hattie was so tiny in stature, it was necessary for her to take several steps back from the gallows, in order to see Ira's face.

Sheriff Sanders slowly placed the noose over Ira's head, around his neck, and adjusted it. Hattie's and Ira's eyes met and at that moment in time, their love, be what it may, was forged in the fires of eternity. Hattie, seeing the look of anxiety on Ira's face, took a long deep breath and reached out for Matthew's hand.

Ira, seeing what happened, smiled. The wind picked up and a dog howled somewhere in the distance. Strangely, Ira felt one particularly intense stare, as he tried to resign himself to his fate. Scanning the crowd, his eyes met Laville's. Standing beside Stanley Johnson, a vengeful smile crossed her face, and he saw her mouthing the words, "Good Riddance, Ira! Burn in Hell!" After which, the hood was placed over his head.

Sheriff Sanders then adjusted the straps about his Ira's wrists and readied himself by the lever. The hood was black and made of heavy material, and with it over his head, Ira could hardly breathe. With everything ready at 11:18 A.M. on December 28, 1899, the signal was given, and with a broken heart, Sheriff Sanders pulled the lever. The hinged platform shot out from under Ira's feet, and his body vaulted downward.

Chapter 8
PEACE AT LAST

HATTIE, HER HEART BREAKING, stood not far from the scaffold when the lever was pulled. Unable to shut her eyes or turn away, she stood wide-eyed and held tightly to Matthew's hand as Ira's body came crashing down to a violent stop at the end of the rope. The crowd stood spellbound, gazing at the ghastly scene that had unfolded before them. Watching with disdain as Ira's limp body swayed in the cold December breeze, the only sound that could be heard was the rope creaking eerily in the silence, and the only movement from Ira's body was when, for brief moments, his hand twitched. For nearly five minutes, this pattern continued, as the entire gallery stood motionless.

Finally, after what seemed like an eternity to Matthew, Ira's body was cut down and the Sheriff called two doctors to come to his side by the body. After a quick examination, he was pronounced dead. Together, the doctors went to Hattie and said that Ira's neck had been broken by the fall, or in other words, his death had been instantaneous. Then, as kindly as possible, they offered their condolences. She nodded, finding it impossible to speak. The words 'thank God it's over' kept tumbling over and over in her mind, like pebbles in a river being washed out to sea.

Next, the Jury and Judge Stepp, as required by law, were summoned forward to examine the body and stated publicly that Ira Saxon was indeed dead.

Turning wearily to Matthew, Hattie gently laid her head against his chest. She needed his support right now, and wrapping her arms around him, Hattie took solace in his loving embrace. Photographers from several large newspapers, who had been taking pictures of Ira's body, took advantage of the moment and began taking pictures of Hattie in Matthew's arms.

"Hattie," Matthew whispered in her ear, "the photographers are having a field day taking pictures of us."

Still in his embrace, she tilted her face upwards. "At this point, I don't care. Stay close, Matthew, I'm going to need you now more than ever."

Looking out over the unending sea of faces, Lou turned to Minerva and said, "Hattie is holding up quite well, but I wonder if she has enough strength to face what's coming in the long hours ahead?"

"She's going to need all of us, Lou," Minerva replied. "Things are going to get ugly fast, and if we don't follow the plan Hattie put together exactly, we won't have a ghost of a chance of containing this crowd."

Turning to walk toward the scaffold, Hattie could see Ira's body was already being moved by the Sheriff's Deputies. It was placed on a slab of lumber and covered with a sheet a mere fifteen feet from the crowd, to be prepared for a special viewing. As Hattie got close to the Ira's body, she glanced over her shoulder to see that the crowd was already pushing its way forward. It was just as she had seen in a dream months earlier, and as she finally stopped next to the slab of lumber, she could hear the vilest words coming from common hoodlums in the crowd. Several others, caught up in this disgusting scene, uttered filthy oaths, and many spat and threw things in the direction of Ira's body.

Ira's sisters screamed out in agony, as they watched these events unfold and forced themselves to the front where they could confront the hoodlums. Cameron and Archer caught them, however, and escorted them along with the rest of the family to their place near Ira.

Knowing time was of the essence, the deputies and Hattie's bodyguards quickly began carrying the plan Hattie had come up with months before, knowing the crowd could cause problems if allowed. First, a wooden chair, on which Hattie would sit, was brought forward and placed near the head of Ira's body, facing the crowd. Secondly, several of Hattie's men picked up benches that had been set out of sight and placed them in a semicircle close behind the chair and the slab on which Ira's body lay. Hattie's men then stood in front of the slab, while several deputies stood behind, in front of the benches. Even to these men of great stamina, the actions of the crowd made them sick to their stomachs. Finally, Sheriff Sanders took his place at the end of Ira's body. The bodyguards, deputies, Hattie's brothers, and the Sheriff all standing shoulder to shoulder in front of the family and Ira created a formidable sight.

Rebecca, Lou, and Lorna, who had gotten separated from the family made their way through the crowd toward Hattie. Mr. Ardmore, the banker, stopped Rebecca momentarily as she walked by and said, "This certainly is a black day in the history of Gallatin, Rebecca. I just heard that over three thousand more people from the surrounding area are waiting outside the enclosure. I'm afraid Miss Hattie is sure going to have her hands full. The enclosure is about to be dismantled and will be laid on the ground. When it is, those on the outside will, no doubt, rush in."

"Hattie and Matthew are prepared for that," Rebecca replied confidently. "They have gone to great pains to assure that everything will go smoothly. Hopefully, there are enough men and deputies to control those who want to do harm."

The crowd, noisy and restless, worried Hattie. Looking to Ira's sisters, Emily and Mary, who were bordering on hysteria, Hattie turned to her mother and said, "Get them out of here, Mama. Bring them back in a few hours when most of the people are gone." Shannon escorted the three of them out of the enclosure, and upon returning, he took his place behind Hattie. Seeing him, she yelled above the ever increasingly noisy crowd. "Come on, Big Brother, I need you."

Nodding, he followed her and Matthew closely as they moved out in front of Ira's body.

Reaching the front, Hattie pulled out her 45's from under her cape, aimed beyond the crowd toward an unpopulated part of the square, and pulled the triggers twice. The crowd fell silent, and those in front of her immediately backed away. "Dear God," she prayed silently, "give me the strength to get through this and conduct myself as a lady." Reaching down and pulling back the sheet that covered Ira's body, Hattie could hardly stomach what she saw. The scene was far more ghastly than any of them had expected. First and most disturbing, Ira's eyes were wide open, staring forward in horror. Then, as if that wasn't bad enough, his hair, which had not been fully covered by the sheet, was covered in spittle. Lastly, his neck, still raw from the rope burn, oozed blood, and his head, due to his broken neck, lay completely off-center. She could hardly stand the sight of Ira in this condition, yet she could hardly look away. Then, from the corner of her eye, she saw Reverend and Mrs. Walker making their way toward her from behind the gallows carrying a pail of warm water, clean cloths, and a comb.

Shannon took hold of Hattie and lovingly moved her away, as Matthew closed Ira's eyes and Mrs. Scarborough, the undertaker's wife, worked with the muscles in Ira's face in an effort to relax them. Reverend and Sister Walker cleaned Ira's clothes, hands, and face and rinsed his hair and combed it. In the meantime, Shannon handed Hattie a bundle that he had been holding for her, containing a small pillow and a sheet made of the same pale blue velvet as her dress. Mrs. Walker and Lou then helped Hattie unfold the sheet of velvet. At the same time, several deputies lifted Ira's body and placed ropes under the slab and around Ira, tying his body down. Mr. Scarborough warned them that in just a matter of hours, rigor mortis would set in, and his body would be quite apt to convulse at that time. The sheet of velvet was then placed over Ira, and the small pillow was placed beneath his head. Reverend Walker and his wife took their prearranged places at the foot of Ira's body, along with the Sheriff and several members of the family, in chairs provided by the deputies. Finally, Hattie took her place again near the chair at Ira's head. With the restoration of Ira's body complete, he now appeared as a dignitary lying in state. Hattie's entourage, who had been shielding all this preparation from view of the spectators, now stepped away and stood behind the now seated deputies.

The enclosure, which had held back thousands of people, had now been dismantled and lay on the ground. Matthew, even though he knew the crowd was enormous, was still amazed at the great number of people rushing toward them. The crowd and photographers were going crazy, as well as the journalists, who were interviewing people and writing as fast as they could.

Seeing the scene before him, Matthew was saddened, thinking that it wasn't Ira's hanging necessarily that had brought all this on but Hattie's notoriety. Because of its very nature, the hanging should have been a solemn occasion, but instead, it had turned into a three-ring circus. Matthew felt Hattie's and Ira's families deserved better.

The area where the scaffolding had been built was on a knoll, and it was as easy for Hattie to view the crowd as it was for the crowd to see her. As she had done before, she fired her revolvers to gain the attention of the spectators. Speaking in as loud a voice as possible, she said, "Now, Ladies and Gentleman, my husband lies here before you. Those of you who can conduct yourselves properly and wish to view my husband's body, I will meet most respectfully, but if anyone comes forward with the express purpose of defiling his body or his reputation in the slightest, I promise, they will be met by my wrath and indignation. Sheriff Sanders, his deputies, and Reverend and Sister Walker will be my witnesses, if such a provocation should arise. My husband is dead and can do nothing to defend himself, but I can. And so help me God, I will do just that!" Sitting down in her chair, Hattie placed her 45's in her lap in plain view, sat erect, smiled, and did her best to appear as a lady.

For the next five hours, thousands of people passed by Ira's body. James and Minerva were proud of Hattie, for she really did present herself as a lady, even with the revolvers lying in her lap. What might have been a complete disaster became, quite amazingly, a scene of dignity and respect. Matthew, Cameron, and Archer were truly in awe of Hattie's gracious manner, in this, her most dire hour.

Laville waited several hours to come forward, but when she did, she began pushing, shoving, and demanding that people move out of her way. Making her way directly to Hattie, she spoke in an indignant tone. "Don't you think for one minute, Hattie that I have come to pay my respects! I just want to make sure that sorry bastard is dead!"

Matthew stepped forward, placed his arm around Laville's waist and gently but firmly took her out of the line. Walking her around the deputies and behind the scaffold, he gently reprimanded her, "I know you're upset, Laville, everyone is, but don't you realize that both sides of the family are devastated and deeply hurt by all of this?" They returned to Hattie and found, to Matthew's great sorrow that Ira's sisters had returned early and had fallen at the feet of their dead brother.

Hattie's and Laville's eyes met and seeing no change in Laville's countenance, Hattie said, "Your heart is as cold as a coward's, Laville." Laville sneered, threw her long raven hair over her shoulder and stormed off.

By five o' clock in the late afternoon, the daylight had left and street lights were being lit around the town square. Minerva gently touched Hattie's hand. "Come, Hattie Dear, we really must leave. We're all half-frozen, and Mr. Scarborough says he must take Ira's body now."

Hattie stood with a heavy heart and slowly turned around to the sheriffs and their deputies. "Gentlemen, you were just wonderful to Ira and me today. I will never, ever forget your kindness." Then, in an effort to show her deep appreciation, she approached each one and thanked them individually.

The horse drawn hearse arrived minutes later, and the deputies lifted Ira's body and placed it inside. Hattie, caught up in talking with her family, didn't realize Ira was being taken away until she heard the wheels in the half-frozen mud. "Wait!" she called loudly. "Wait just a minute." The hearse rolled to a stop. "I have a bag with the clothes I want Ira to be buried in. It's there in my carriage."

Matthew called out, "I'll get it for you, Hattie." He jumped over as much mud as he could to a place that was frozen and grabbed the bag from her carriage. "Here it is," he said, handing it to Mr. Scarborough.

Hattie added, "If there is a problem, Mr. Scarborough, you can contact me. I will be at Judge Stepp's home tonight. Please be careful with the suit. I had it made especially for Ira, and it's all white."

As the hearse rolled away, the wind picked up and a few scattered raindrops began to fall. Sheriff Sanders walked over to Hattie and took her hands. "Well, Little Lady, everythin' is ready for tomorrow. The boys and I will be ready at ten o' clock for the funeral tomorrow

mornin', and I'll have deputies posted at the funeral parlor all night."
Taking her aside, he put his arm around her. "Miss Hattie you were
completely right about this all along. Havin' all of us here as a united
front was the right thin' for Ira. God only knows what kind of an affair
this might have turned out to be if we hadn't been."

"Thank you, Sheriff, you've been more than kind. Now that it's all
over, do you mind if I ask you something personal?"

"No, Ma'am, of course not."

"I was wondering why it was you who pulled the lever instead of a
deputy?"

He sighed heavily. "What I did, Miss Hattie, I did in love. I knew
that someone had to do it, and I want you to know that it was the hardest thin' that I've ever done. Feelin' as I did about him, I just couldn't
let another man send him into the next world."

With Matthew at her side, Hattie climbed into her carriage and rode
away from the town square with her entourage following close behind.
Turning, she looked one last time at the gallows, and the starkness of
the wooden structure against the darkening sky caused her to shudder.

Matthew worried about her state of mind and said lovingly, "Hattie,
regardless of what has happened here today you must not let it canker
your soul."

"I won't let that happen, Matthew, but I know without a doubt that
I'll never be free of this memory."

Judge Stepp and his family stood outside the front door waiting for
Hattie, Matthew, and her men to arrive. It had been the Judge himself
who invited Hattie, Matthew, and her men to spend the night in his
home. Hattie worried about her men being comfortable with all that
had happened that day, as they too had been under great emotional
strain. After they brought in their bedrolls, she spoke with them at

length, once again telling them of her great love and respect for them. The men were grateful, not only for her love, but for her generosity. Encouraging her not to worry, Matthew said, "Remember, Hattie, we're men, not little boys. We'll be just fine."

As she sat on the edge of her bed that night, she gazed at the clouds moving swiftly across the moonlit sky. The freezing rain had stopped, but there was a definite change coming in the weather. The streaks of lightning in the distance were evidence of it. Winter lightning storms always made her uneasy, as there had always been something evil and foreboding about them. Laying her head on her pillow, she tried to erase the horrible events of the day from her mind, but as try she might, she kept reliving the scene of Ira's body hanging from the gallows, swinging limply in the breeze. Desperately, she wondered if any other thought would ever force that horrible scene from her mind.

By morning, the streets were full of slush. In the night, the freezing rain had started up again, turned to snow, and finally back to rain, before finally letting up at dawn. Hattie dressed, and upon opening her bedroom door, she found Matthew waiting. They greeted each other and walked downstairs in silence to breakfast.

An hour later, they met with Mr. Scarborough at the funeral parlor, and seeing Ira's body, Hattie was amazed at the miracle the undertaker and his wife had managed to accomplish with his face. Looking down at him, he didn't appear dead as he did the day before, but instead, he looked to only be sleeping. The look of peace on his face brought an immediate sense of relief to Hattie. As she stood alone looking at him, she felt a soft breeze enter the room, as if the front door to the funeral parlor had opened, then closed. She thought she heard a woman walk up beside her and stand quietly. At first, she assumed it was her mother or Lou. Yet, when she turned to see who was there, she was shocked to find no one at all. Then, quite peculiarly, a delicate fragrance filled the air. It was the scent of lilacs, the same scent she remembered Ira's mother Samantha wearing. Smiling to herself, Hattie took solace in knowing that Ira was finally at peace and reunited with those most dear to him.

The ride to the cemetery was the longest ride Hattie had ever known. She had asked Rachel Stepp, the Judge's daughter, to ride in the carriage with her and Matthew, but little was said between them. Rachel knew Hattie had her family, but realized she needed a girlfriend now. Matthew was grateful that the services at the church had been uneventful. Only family and close friends were invited and the crowd outside, although enormous, had remained relatively quiet.

The day was dreary and cold, and at the grave site, Hattie stood at the head of Ira's casket, numb of all feeling. As Reverend Walker was speaking, her mind wandered back to the week of her honeymoon. She recalled how, from the very beginning, the time she and Ira spent together seemed to be filled with quarreling and dissention. "How and why did everything have to go so wrong?" she wondered.

Finally, her mother touched her arm gently, awakening her from her thoughts. "Hattie, Hattie Dear, set your flowers on the casket. It's time to leave."

Carefully, she laid them down and looked toward the road that led to the cemetery. She could hardly believe what she saw, as the road was lined on both sides with hundreds of carriages and buggies, for at least a mile in both directions. Whispering to Mr. Scarborough, she asked, "This casket is filled with dirt and rocks, isn't it?"

He smiled and nodded. "Yes it is, Hattie. We moved Ira to Silver Creek on the back roads during the funeral services just like you wanted."

Hattie breathed a sigh of relief. Seeing the crowd the day before, she had felt sure that Ira's grave would be desecrated. Hattie and Shannon had chosen a secret place on the estate in the woods for his actual burial. He would be buried later in the day, unbeknownst to anyone but the family.

That evening the entire family (excluding Laville) stood in a quiet grove at Silver Creek. The service was simple, and as everyone returned to the mansion, Mr. Scarborough and his wife finished with Ira's burial. It had been a long and difficult day, but Hattie could at last rest with a semblance of peace. It was comforting to know that Ira's final resting place was a guarded secret.

The next morning, Mr. Scarborough returned to the estate and confirmed Hattie's greatest fear. "Miss Hattie, I hate to tell you this, even though you expected it. The grave at the cemetery was dug up in the night, and the coffin brought out, opened, and overturned. Of course the grave robbers found nothing but earth and rocks in the casket, but I shudder to think what might have happened had we buried Ira there as was originally planned."

Matthew, Rebecca, Lou, and Minerva sat in the parlor with Hattie listening to Mr. Scarborough. Then, walking the kindly old man to the door, Matthew said to the undertaker gratefully, "We can't thank you enough, Mr. Scarborough, for all your help."

"It's been my pleasure, Mr. Forsythe. I've known both Ira and Hattie since they were children." He paused. "And I thought the world of Andrew and Samantha. Ira may have had his faults, but I'll never believe he killed Nick Starr, let alone in cold blood." With that, he shook Matthew's hand firmly and said goodbye.

Standing at the door for a long time, Matthew watched the undertaker's carriage until it reached the main road. He then returned to the parlor and overheard Lou talking to Hattie.

"It seems the cards were stacked against Ira from the start, Hattie, and they were fanned into a fiery blaze by the hate in the hearts of the people of Gallatin. Unfortunate as it is, I'm afraid Ira never had a chance."

"I'll never be able to rest, Lou," Hattie replied somberly. "Not until I find out who killed Nick and why."

Mary, who just entered the room as well, spoke up with uneasiness in her voice. "Best you be leavin' all of it at the feet of the Almighty, Lass. It be over now, and I be thinkin' it be best if you just be a puttin' it in the past. Many a time me George be sayin', 'It not always be best to be knowin' everythin' cause sometimes it be a mite more than a body can stand'."

Minerva, although heartsick over the events of the past day, felt now was the time to try to give Hattie some real encouragement. Walking to her daughter, who stood silently gazing into the fireplace, she pointed to the heavens and said, "Take heart in knowing the Almighty is watching over us, Dear. You have your whole life to look forward to, and believe me, none of us knows what is written in the stars."

Stepping up behind Hattie as well, Matthew added, "Ira gave me the book he was writing, the poems, his Bible, and this note. Perhaps it might give you some solace."

"Read it to me, please," she asked politely.

"The note reads, 'Hattie, fear not what the future holds, I am at 'peace at last'. Read Psalms 91:11'." Putting down the note and opening up the Bible, he waited for everyone to gather around then said, "It reads, 'For he shall give his angels charge over thee'."

"You know, Matthew," Hattie said softly, "even when you love someone dearly, you still make mistakes."

Handing the Bible to Minerva, Matthew opened up his arms to

Hattie, and they embraced each other tenderly in front of the fireplace. Standing silent, Minerva, Rebecca, and Lou hoped beyond a hope that Hattie would somehow be able to overcome this chapter of her life. Then, as they watched Hattie lay her head on Matthew's massive chest, while illuminated perfectly by the soft glow of the fire behind them, time, for a moment, stood still, and they remembered, all too well, a timeless pearl of wisdom: 'sometimes the worst thing that happens - is also the best.' Glancing toward the flames dancing rhythmically in the fireplace, Hattie knew God was purging her by taking out the impurities of her life in 'the fires of love and hate', and standing silent in Matthew's arms, all Hattie could hear was the beating of his heart.

About the Author

ALEX SKYLER ALEXANDER is a bright, motivated thirty five year old male who has been working on a novel which was the combined effort between him and his late father Shayne Alexander. Forced to Love is the first in a series of novels about the very colorful life of Sky's great-grandmother, Hattie.

For more information about Sky Alexander make sure to check out his website and signup for his free News Letter with special deals only to only the select member.

http://www.risingphoenixinc.net

Also check out Sky Alexander Facebook Page
https://www.facebook.com/pages/Rising-Phoenix-Inc/917717931591630

The Fires of Love & Hate

Book 1 Forced to Love	Released	Sky Alexander
Book 2 Falling into Love	Released	Sky Alexander
Book 3 Hate to Love	Released	Sky Alexander
Book 4 Death of Love	Released	Sky Alexander
Book 5 Romancing the Heart	Pending Release	Sky Alexander
Book 6 Whirl Wind Romance	Pending Release	Sky Alexander
Book 7 Forgiving Romance	Pending Release	Sky Alexander
Book 8 Broken Promises	Pending Release	Sky Alexander
Book 9 Shattered Dreams	Pending Release	Sky Alexander
Book 10 The Price of Intrigue	Pending Release	Sky Alexander
Book 11 On a Course with Destiny	Pending Release	Sky Alexander
Book 12 Confessions of the Heart	Pending Release	Sky Alexander
Book 13 Dead or Alive	Writing	Sky Alexander
Book 14 Angel Tears	Under Development	Sky Alexander
Book 15 Forgiveness	Under Development	Sky Alexander
Book 16 Breaking the Cycle	Under Development	Sky Alexander
Book 17 The Promise of Life	Under Development	Sky Alexander
Book 18 Eternity for a Moment	Under Development	Sky Alexander
Book 19 Before the Sun Goes Down	Under Development	Sky Alexander
Book 20 Rising like a Phoenix	Under Development	Sky Alexander

Action Adventure/ Thriller
Aspen Falls

Book 1 Throw Words to the Wind	Pending Release	Sky Alexander
Book 2 No Blame for Ascending	Pending Release	Sky Alexander
Book 3 Like an Infidel Sea	Pending Release	Sky Alexander
Book 4 The Lost City of Atheria	Pending Release	Sky Alexander
Book 5 My Dreams Could be Tomorrow	Pending Release	Sky Alexander

Book 6 Some Feelings Never Die	Pending Release	Sky Alexander
Book 7 A Head Filled with Doubt	Pending Release	Sky Alexander
Book 8 Sea of Waking Dreams	Writing	Sky Alexander
Book 9 Unreal	Under Development	Sky Alexander
Book 10 Where the River Flows	Under Development	Sky Alexander
Book 11 A Whisper of Truth	Under Development	Sky Alexander
Book 12 Washed Away Dreams	Under Development	Sky Alexander
Book 13 Choices Haunting the Future	Under Development	Sky Alexander
Book 14 My Apology	Under Development	Sky Alexander
Book 15 River of Tears	Under Development	Sky Alexander

Vampire Series
World of Darkness

Book 1 War of Angels	Writing	Sky Alexander
Book 2 A Prophecy of the Future	Under Development	Sky Alexander
Book 3 Rise of Two Families	Under Development	Sky Alexander
Book 4 Holy Fire	Under Development	Sky Alexander
Book 5 Dark Beginnings	Under Development	Sky Alexander
Book 6 The Final Battle	Under Development	Sky Alexander

www.ingramcontent.com/pod-product-compliance
Lightning Source LLC
Chambersburg PA
CBHW070602180626
46817CB00005B/1958